Ashen Oath

Zora Stone

Print ISBN: 978-1-971405-06-3

Publisher: Smut by Design

www.zorastone.com

To the endings that open into beginnings, and the clarity born of reflection.

Previously in the Ether Chronicles

A quick refresher before we dive into the sacred and the shattered

Hey there, lovely readers! Ready to return to Bree's world? Here's what you need to remember before everything gets complicated:

Crown of the Mist: Bree survived alone in a crappy apartment while silver mist stalked her like a magical pet. Her five childhood friends pined dramatically from a distance until her creepy landlord Phil got handsy. Bree's power exploded (very satisfying), she touched a mysterious crown, everything went white, and boom—magic is real and she's apparently royalty. Classic Tuesday.

Into the Ether: Enter Thane—gorgeous, dangerous, and definitely not human. He arrived to investigate Bree for the Council but got distracted by her accidentally rebuilding an entire magical sanctuary. The place literally reshaped itself around her, magical refugees started showing up, and Stellan appeared to provide sarcastic commentary and suspicious amounts of helpful information.

Bree's awakening changed everyone around her too—the guys are all developing their own magical abilities, glowing slightly, and looking unfairly attractive. Meanwhile, the Council is circling closer, Phil is still lurking somewhere being genuinely terrifying, and Seth has been quietly walking the gardens being... helpful. Maybe too helpful.

Everything seemed to be falling into place until Thane overheard a phone call that made his blood run cold. Because apparently, someone's been playing a much longer game than anyone realized.

And that someone might be closer than they think.

Welcome to *Ashen Oath*.

Hope you're ready for ancient mirror magic, impossible choices, and the kind of revelations that make you question everything you thought you knew about the people you trust.

(Fair warning: Things are about to get *very* messy.)

Trigger Warnings

Thank you for reading *Ashen Oath*. This book contains themes and content that may be triggering to some readers. Please review the following warnings before proceeding:

Emotional & Psychological Themes

- **Betrayal & Trust Issues** – Major revelations about trusted characters; emotional manipulation

- **Identity Crisis & Self-Doubt** – Questioning reality, worth, and personal identity

- **Psychological Manipulation** – Gaslighting, coercion, and emotional control by antagonistic forces

- **PTSD & Trauma Responses** – Ongoing processing of abuse, panic attacks, dissociation

- **Corruption & Mental Influence** – Magical/supernatural manipulation of thoughts and emotions

- **Abandonment & Rejection** – Fear of being left behind; withdrawal from loved ones

Violence & Supernatural Threats

- **Physical Confrontations** – Magical battles, physical attacks, restraint against will

- **Blood & Injury** – Vampire feeding, magical wounds, physical harm

- **Supernatural Horror** – Void realm encounters, otherworldly entities, reality distortion

- **Stalking & Pursuit** – Being hunted by dangerous magical beings

- **Death & Loss** – Character deaths, grief, mourning

Intimacy & Relationships

- **Explicit Sexual Content** – Detailed intimate scenes between adults

- **Polyamorous Dynamics** – Multiple romantic/sexual relationships, complex emotional bonds

- **Magical Bonding** – Soul-deep connections with permanent consequences

- **Consent & Agency** – Exploration of choice under magical influence

- **Relationship Strain** – Conflict, miscommunication, protective withdrawal

Dark Magic & Supernatural Elements

- **Magical Corruption** – Power being tainted or used harmfully

- **Reality Distortion** – Mirrors, alternate selves, questioning what's real

- **Ancient Magic & Rituals** – Dangerous ceremonies with life-altering consequences

- **Supernatural Possession/Influence** – External forces affecting behavior and choices

- **Void/Dark Realm Encounters** – Otherworldly spaces, existential horror

Family & Authority

- **Parental Abuse References** – Continued impact of childhood trauma

- **Power Imbalances** – Political manipulation, magical hierarchy, coercion

- **Governmental/Council Oppression** – Surveillance, control, persecution of magical beings

This list is provided to ensure a safe reading experience. If any of these topics are personally distressing, please read with care and compassion for yourself.

Thank you for continuing this journey with Bree and her chosen family.

Zora Stone

CONTENTS

Chapter 1
BREE

Sleep isn't happening.

I've tried every position, counted sheep, even attempted some deep breathing thing Theo taught me once. Nothing works. Every time I close my eyes, my brain cycles through everything—what happened with Thane in the garden, Theo's panicked vision, the way he looked so shaken. And poor Seth caught in the middle of it all.

I should have found Theo when I came back inside. Should have made sure he was okay. But by the time Thane and I... by the time we came back from the garden, he was nowhere to be found, and asking the others felt like admitting I'd failed him somehow.

So now I'm lying here replaying the way Thane's hands felt on my skin. The way he said my name when his fangs found my throat. The way the bond snapped into place between us, silver and warm and permanent.

Like forever. That kind of permanent.

And the way I walked away from Theo when he needed me, because apparently I'm excellent at letting people down.

What are the others going to think? The thought hits me like ice water. I spent years pushing them all away, convincing myself it was safer for everyone if I kept my distance. Then I finally let them close, and the first thing I do is... this. With Thane. With someone who was supposed to be watching me for the Council.

Did I just screw up everything we were building here? Everything I thought we were building?

My chest tightens. Will they think I chose him over them? Will they decide this is too complicated, too messy, too much? Maybe this will be the thing that finally makes them walk away.

I press my palms against my eyes, trying to stop the spiral. But the fear sits there, cold and familiar.

You don't have to be whole to be worthy of being seen.

Theo's words from the living room float back to me. When everything had just fallen apart and I thought I'd lost them all. When he looked at me like I mattered, broken pieces and all.

I have to believe they'll stick around no matter who I end up with. I have to believe that what we've built together is stronger than my fears.

Even if I'm not sure I believe it yet.

I roll over for the hundredth time, burying my face in pillows that smell like lavender and starlight. The sanctuary bedroom should feel like peace—with its curved walls and silver script that pulses gently in the moonlight streaming through the dome above. Everything here was built for comfort.

Instead, I feel like I'm vibrating out of my skin.

That's when I notice it.

The mirror from the garden sits on the bedside table where I left it before crawling into bed. The same twisted silver frame with spirals and curves that flow into sharp points like horns or antlers. The surface that drinks light instead of reflecting it properly, ancient and hungry.

I should leave it alone. After what I saw earlier—my eyes glowing red, then going completely black. Both Seth and Thane seemed uneasy about it too. I should probably throw the damn thing out a window.

Instead, I reach for it.

The metal is warm under my fingers, and I can't tell if that's from my own body heat or something else entirely. Something that makes my pulse quicken.

My reflection stares back, all messy hair and wide eyes. Pretty standard post-crisis look for me. But as I tilt it to catch the moonlight, something shifts.

The surface ripples.

I blink hard, wondering if I'm finally losing it. But when I look again, I'm not seeing myself anymore.

I'm seeing the corridor from earlier.

The scene plays out in perfect detail, but from an angle I never had. I watch myself move toward Thane, silver mist trailing behind me like a living thing. But there are details I missed—the way the Ether reaches for him before I'm even close, wrapping around his boots like it's claiming territory.

And his face when he thinks I'm not looking. Less controlled. More raw.

Like he's seeing something he wants and dreads in equal measure.

My heart does something complicated as I watch the scene unfold. When mirror-me brushes past him, I swear I feel the ghost of that contact. But it's what happens next that makes me sit up straighter.

A thread of silver light passes between us where the Ether touched him. Just for a heartbeat—a connection that glows like captured starlight.

I didn't see that. Couldn't have seen it.

"What the hell?" I whisper.

The image ripples again, and suddenly I'm looking at Thane alone in ruins. Cracked stone walls, pale light filtering through broken spaces. He's kneeling before what looks like a scrying mirror, and silver mist is rising from its shattered edges—my Ether, somehow reaching across distance.

He's pressing his hand to his chest, right over his heart, and his expression is completely unguarded. Stunned. Like his entire world just shifted and he doesn't know which way is up anymore.

Like he's just realized I've been here all along.

The scene fades, leaving me staring at my own reflection again. But now I look different—pupils dilated, breathing shallow. Like I've just seen something I wasn't supposed to.

I set the mirror down, my hands not quite steady. "Okay. Either I'm having a breakdown, or you're showing me things that actually happened."

The sigils around the frame pulse once, faint but deliberate.

"Great. Of course you are."

Against every instinct I have, I pick it up again. Because apparently I never learn.

This time, when the surface ripples, I'm looking at the sanctuary again. But wrong.

The main hall stretches out before me, its familiar curved walls and silver script. Except something's off. The script still glows, but it feels hollow somehow, like an echo of warmth rather than warmth itself. And I'm there, but not me. This version stands frozen in the center while the boys reach for her with desperate hands.

Rhett, Jace, Gray, Theo, Wes, Thane—and others behind them, faces I can almost recognize—but their faces are twisted with something between hunger and panic. And she's backing away from them, the Ether around her feet gone black as spilled ink.

Behind them all, barely visible in the shadows, stands someone I don't recognize. Tall, watching, with an intensity that makes my skin prickle.

The other-me opens her mouth like she's trying to speak, but no sound comes through the glass. The black Ether spreads outward from her feet, and everyone it touches—

I jerk the mirror away from my face, heart hammering against my ribs.

"Okay, that's enough of that."

I set it down more carefully this time, but I can't stop staring at it. The frame glows faintly in the moonlight, keeping time with my pulse.

Outside, footsteps echo in the corridor—someone doing a final check before bed. The normalcy of it should be comforting. Instead, it makes me think of that other version of myself, reaching for something I couldn't quite see.

I grab the blanket and pull it over my head like that'll help. But even with my eyes closed, I can feel the mirror's presence. Waiting. Watching.

Just another glamorous night in paradise, I think, borrowing my own sarcasm for comfort.

But it doesn't help. My heart won't stop racing, and every time I close my eyes, I see that other version of myself with the black Ether spreading around her feet. Not evil—just different. Wrong in a way I can't name.

A faint scent drifts through the room—chamomile and something sweeter, like honey and vanilla. I sit up, frowning, and find a steaming mug on the nightstand beside the mirror.

It wasn't there before. I'm sure of it.

The sanctuary, I realize. Paying attention to what I need before I know I need it, just like always.

I reach for the mug, careful not to touch the mirror, and wrap my hands around the warm ceramic. The tea tastes like comfort and safety, like being held when the world gets too sharp around the edges. Just how Wes usually makes it—sweet, careful, like he knows what I need before I do.

My pulse slows. The terror in my chest eases to something manageable.

"Thank you," I whisper to the room, and the silver script on the walls pulses once, gentle as a heartbeat.

I finish the tea and set the mug back down. The calm should carry me straight into sleep.

It doesn't.

My brain keeps circling back to what I saw. That silver thread between Thane and me. The other sanctuary that felt hollow. My mirror-self with black Ether pooling around her feet.

I shift under the blankets, listening to the quiet. The tea helped, but didn't erase everything. I'm tired but not settled, balanced on that knife's edge where sleep might happen if I stop thinking.

Good luck with that.

A soft knock interrupts the silence. Deliberate, but not urgent. Not hesitant either.

I freeze. Maybe it's Theo, still shaken from his vision. Or Wes, drawn by whatever restless energy he's been carrying lately. But something about the rhythm feels different.

The door opens just enough for someone to slip through.

Stellan.

He stands in the doorway like he's waiting for permission to exist in the same space as me. Moonlight catches the sharp line of his jaw, but I can't read his expression from here.

He doesn't move closer. Doesn't speak. Just... waits.

There's a question in his stillness that I don't entirely understand. But somehow, I know what he's asking.

I tilt my head at him.

He crosses the room like he's done this before, but careful. No assumptions. When he reaches the bed, he pauses again.

"Okay?" he asks, voice barely above a whisper.

I nod.

He climbs onto the bed with that fluid grace of his, settling behind me without crowding. When his arm slides around my waist, I stiffen—because that's what I do—but he just murmurs, "Shh," once, low and calm.

His hold is loose. Present, but not possessive.

The knot in my chest starts to loosen. My breathing shifts to match his without me deciding to. The sharp edges that the tea couldn't quite reach begin to blur.

"How?" I whisper.

He's quiet for so long I think he won't answer. When he finally speaks, his voice is soft against my hair.

"Your peace matters more than what it costs me."

I should probably ask what he means. Should wonder what this is costing him.

Instead, I let myself sink back against him.

Whatever his magic is doing, it's working. The anxious spiral in my head slows, then stops. My eyelids get heavy in a way that feels natural instead of forced.

The visions from the mirror fade to background noise—still there, but manageable. Like turning down the volume on a song that was too loud.

The last thing I'm aware of is his steady breathing and the way his presence makes the room feel safer. Just as I'm drifting off, his arm tightens around me—barely, but enough that I feel it. Like he's anchoring me to something solid.

The last conscious thought I have is still wondering if that dark vision was a warning or a promise.

But at least now I'm not wondering alone.

Chapter 2
RHETT

The sanctuary feels different when she's sleeping.

Not quieter—the stone walls still hum with that gentle silver glow, and the guys are making enough noise in the main room to wake half the magical world. But there's something settled about the air now that Bree's finally resting. Like the whole place exhales when she stops carrying the weight of everything on her shoulders.

I hover in the hallway outside her door longer than I should, listening for any sign of restlessness. After everything that happened yesterday—Theo's vision especially—I wouldn't be surprised if she was still awake.

Silence. Deep, exhausted silence.

My hand is already on the doorknob before I realize what I'm doing. Just a quick check, I tell myself. Make sure she's okay.

I push the door open an inch.

She's curled on her side, breathing slow and even. Stellan's there too—stretched out behind her, his arm draped over her—

What the hell is Stellan doing in her bed?

Heat flares up my spine. My hands clench before I can stop them. Every muscle in my body coils, ready to storm in there and drag him away from her.

The smell of heated metal cuts through my rage. I look down—the doorknob is glowing faintly under my grip, heat radiating through the brass. Before I can even let go, cool silver light flows down from the doorframe, and the metal cools beneath my palm.

The sanctuary. Keeping me from burning the place down.

I force myself to look back at her. At them.

She looks... peaceful. More peaceful than I've seen her in weeks.

Damn it.

I close the door, jaw tight enough to crack teeth.

She's finally asleep. That's what matters.

I make myself walk away, following voices toward the main room where the others have gathered. The space has arranged itself around our presence like it's anticipating something—comfortable seating in a loose circle, warm light glowing from fixtures that weren't there yesterday, the faint scent of something like cedar and starlight.

Jace is already sprawled across one of the couches, a wooden board balanced on his knees loaded with what looks like half of Mairen's kitchen. Cheese, bread, some kind of preserved fruit that gleams like jewels in the light.

"Kitchen lady priorities," he says around a mouthful of something that makes his eyes roll back. "I swear she thinks we're all about to waste away."

"Maybe because you inhaled three servings at dinner and came back for more," Theo points out from his chair. He's got a book open in his lap, but his eyes aren't moving across the page. Just staring at the same spot like his mind's somewhere else entirely.

"Growing boy," Jace says with zero shame. "Besides, carbs are a love language. This is basically a hug you can eat."

Wes hovers near the food like he's torn between wanting and restraint. There's something restless in the way he moves—not the usual hunger I've gotten used to, but something sharper. More aware. Like his whole body's tuned to a frequency the rest of us can't hear.

Gray leans against the far wall, arms crossed, watching all of us with that quiet intensity of his. Not uncomfortable, just observing. Taking the temperature of the room.

And I get it. We're all keyed up, pretending to wind down when really we're just waiting for the next thing to go sideways. It's been that kind of week.

Stellan hasn't joined us yet. I try not to think about where he is.

"She's finally asleep," I say, settling into the chair closest to the hallway. Just in case.

"About time," Jace mutters. "Bree looked like she was running on fumes and stubbornness."

"Can you blame her?" Gray's voice carries an edge. "After everything yesterday—"

"She handled it," Theo says quietly. "Better than any of us would have."

There's truth in that. The way she stood in front of that crowd, called the Ether without flinching, made space and shelter for people she'd never met because they needed it—I've never seen anything like it.

But I also saw the way she swayed afterward. The careful way she held herself, like she was afraid of falling apart if she moved too fast.

"Still," I say, heat flickering under my skin without my permission. "She shouldn't have to—"

The door opens, cutting off whatever protective instinct was about to spill out of my mouth.

Thane steps inside, and something in the room's energy shifts immediately.

It's not obvious at first. He looks like Thane—same controlled posture, same silver eyes that see too much, same dark clothes that make him blend into shadows. But there's something different in the way he moves. A looseness in his shoulders that wasn't there yesterday. A subtle ease that makes the dangerous edge of him seem less like a knife and more like a flame.

Fed, my brain supplies, and I don't know why that word comes to mind.

But before I can place what's changed, Stellan enters the room and goes completely still.

My jaw clenches the second I see him. Heat prickles under my skin—the memory of finding him in her bed flashing through my mind like a brand.

But he's not looking at me. His focus is locked entirely on Thane, and there's something about his stillness that makes my anger shift to unease.

Not human-still. Predator-still. The kind of motionless that means every instinct just snapped to attention.

Jace is still talking about something, gesturing with a piece of bread, but my focus narrows to Stellan's face. The way his gray eyes track over Thane—once, quickly, then again slower. Taking inventory.

Then Stellan smiles.

It starts small, just a quirk at the corner of his mouth. But it spreads, disbelief and amusement and something that looks almost like pride mixing together until he's grinning like he just witnessed a miracle.

"You son of a bitch."

The words drop into the room like stones into still water. Conversation dies instantly. Theo's book snaps shut. Wes freezes mid-reach for another piece of cheese. Gray straightens from the wall.

Stellan chuckles as he crosses the room with that too-smooth stride of his. When he reaches Thane, he claps him on the back—friendly on the surface, but there's weight behind it. Like a test.

Thane doesn't flinch, but something flickers across his face. Color. Actual color, rising along his sharp cheekbones like he's—

Like he's blushing.

Thane doesn't blush. Ever. In the time I've known him, I've never seen him show that kind of reaction to anything.

"Okay," I say, standing up because suddenly this feels like something I need to be ready for. "What the hell is going on?"

Thane's jaw ticks. "Nothing."

"Everything," Stellan says at the same time, and his voice carries a note I've never heard before. Something between amazement and satisfaction. "Absolutely everything."

He takes a step back from Thane, but his eyes never leave his face. Reading something there that the rest of us are missing.

"You've been fed," he says, voice dropping lower. "Properly. And not just fed—"

The pause stretches, loaded with implications I can feel but don't understand.

"Bonded."

The word hits the room like all the air's been sucked out.

Gray straightens completely from the wall, tension coiling through his frame. Theo's book falls forgotten to the floor. Wes goes so still he could be carved from stone.

Jace breaks the silence first, because of course he does.

"Well, shit."

My mind races, trying to process what Stellan's implying. Bonding isn't casual—not for Feeders, and definitely not with anyone magical. It's not something that just happens by accident, not something you walk away from unchanged.

"Who?" Wes asks, voice barely above a whisper.

Thane's jaw ticks. He doesn't answer.

Stellan's smirk widens. "Oh, I think you know." His gaze flicks meaningfully toward the ceiling. "I can smell her on you. Sweet vanilla and starlight."

Bree.

The words hit me like ice water.

Of course it's Bree.

Gray's hands clench into fists at his sides. "You bonded with her?" His voice is deadly quiet.

I look at Thane—really look at him—and suddenly everything makes sense. The loose shoulders, the subtle ease, the way he's standing there like he finally found something worth fighting for.

Theo's gone completely still in his chair.

His eyes have gone distant, unfocused, that familiar glassy look that means he's seeing something the rest of us aren't. His hands grip the arms of his chair, knuckles white.

Then his gaze snaps to mine, clear and certain and somehow ancient.

"It's meant," he says quietly.

The words land in the silence like a benediction. Or a judgment.

"What does that mean?" I ask, but my voice sounds far away.

Stellan chuckles, dark and knowing. "It means our vampire friend here just got himself permanently tethered to the most powerful magical being in existence." His gaze flicks between Thane and the rest of us. "Congratulations. You're all going to have to share."

Thane doesn't deny it. Doesn't confirm it either. Just stands there with that faint flush still visible along his cheekbones, silver eyes daring any of us to make this a problem.

But it's not anger I see in his expression. It's something rawer. More vulnerable.

Like he's waiting for us to tell him he doesn't deserve it.

The silence stretches, heavy with questions none of us know how to ask. Above us, Bree sleeps on, unaware that the room downstairs just got turned completely upside down.

Whatever happened between them last night, it's not nothing.

It's going to change everything.

And I still need to figure out why the fuck Stellan was in her room this morning.

Chapter 3
GRAY

The air in the main room feels thick enough to cut.

Not just because of what Stellan dropped on us—though Thane being bonded to Bree is still sitting in my chest like a stone. It's the way everyone's sitting now, careful distances maintained, avoiding eye contact with Thane like he might bite if they look too long.

Everyone except Wes, who keeps glancing at him and then catching himself.

Stellan's settled into his chair like he's been there all night, relaxed as a cat in a sunbeam. But I know predators. The watchfulness never really leaves, even when they're pretending to nap.

Rhett's too still. That's what catches my attention first—he's always moving, shifting, drumming fingers or bouncing his leg. Now he's locked in place, arms folded tight across his chest, jaw set like he's biting down on words that want to escape. When Stellan's name comes up, Rhett's mouth opens like he's about to say something, then snaps shut. His gaze flicks toward the hallway once, quick and sharp, then back to the floor.

Something's eating at him beyond the obvious.

Thane breaks the silence first, which surprises me. I expected Jace to crack a joke or Theo to offer some philosophical insight. Instead, it's the vampire who clears his throat and starts talking—not about the bond, but about magic.

"Her power is accelerating," he says, voice carefully neutral. "The Ether responds to her without conscious intent now. Physical changes to the sanctuary, objects shifting in response to her emotions." He pauses, silver eyes scanning the room. "The restoration happening here—it's faster than anything I've seen. And it's because she's here."

"So what happens if she leaves?" Wes blurts out, then immediately looks like he wishes he could take it back.

No one answers right away. That question sits in the room like a live grenade.

Rhett's watching Thane through narrowed eyes—not suspicious, exactly, but like he's putting pieces together and doesn't like the picture they're making.

"We all know what this is," Theo says quietly, leaning forward in his chair. He doesn't say *vision*, but there's that Seer certainty in his voice that means he's seen something. "We're all tied to her now. Magic's making it stronger. If we can't get past the pissing matches and figure out how to make it work, it's going to break before it bonds."

Jace nods, surprisingly serious. "He's right. And it won't be her fault when it happens."

Wes stays quiet, but his shoulders are tense. He glances at Stellan, then away again—and there's something in that look I can't quite read. Not anger, but discomfort mixed with something possessive.

That's when I catch it—the smallest flicker of eye contact between Thane and Wes. Silent. Loaded. Gone before I can interpret it, but it leaves me uneasy.

Something's going on there.

Rhett's head turns at the exact same moment, like he noticed it too. But he looks away quickly, lips pressed in a thin line.

"The Council knows about the surge," Thane continues, his voice cutting through my observations. "They felt it everywhere. They know it came from this realm." He pauses, and for the first time since I've known him, he looks almost... uncertain. "I was sent to assess her. But that's not what I'm doing now."

"What are you doing?" I ask.

"Trying to keep her alive." The words are flat, matter-of-fact. "They won't stop until they have her or destroy her. And after the meeting I got pulled into last night—" He stops himself, jaw ticking. "They're sending Phil."

"They're not touching her," Jace says immediately, with a fierceness that surprises no one.

Thane gives him the faintest smirk—almost approval—but doesn't comment.

That's when Zira walks in.

She strolls into the middle of our crisis completely unbothered, heads straight for Jace, and plucks the piece of bread right out of his hand. Takes a bite, chews thoughtfully, then looks around at all of us with raised eyebrows.

"You boys look like someone died," she says around the bread. "What'd I miss?"

Jace glares at her. "That was mine."

"Was being the operative phrase." She takes another bite, ignoring his outrage completely.

The tension breaks for a moment—just a moment—but no one actually answers her question. She wanders over to the food table, still snacking, apparently content to figure it out herself.

"There's more you need to know," Thane says once she's out of immediate earshot. His voice drops lower, more urgent. "I overheard something last night that could change everything. About Seth—"

The scream cuts through the sanctuary like a blade.

Raw. Terrified. Unmistakably Bree.

I'm moving before the sound fully registers, chair crashing behind me as I bolt for the door. Rhett's already there, Wes right beside him, but I'm close enough to feel the heat radiating off Rhett's skin—his fire responding to the fear in her voice.

"Her room," Thane says, appearing at my shoulder with that unsettling vampire speed. His controlled mask has cracked completely, silver eyes sharp with something that looks almost like panic.

We rush through the corridors, footsteps echoing off stone. Zira's voice carries behind us, muttering something that sounds like "really, really bad" between breaths.

The hallway curves ahead, and there's only one door that matters—the one with silver mist seeping underneath like smoke from a fire.

Rhett reaches it first, doesn't bother knocking. The door slams open under his hand.

And we freeze.

Bree's on the floor beside her bed, knees drawn to her chest, whole body shaking like she's been struck by lightning. The mist isn't just leaking—it's pouring off her in waves, thick enough to taste metal on my tongue.

But it's her eyes that stop my heart.

Wide. Terrified. And completely, utterly vacant.

Like she's seeing something none of us can see. Something that's tearing her apart from the inside.

Chapter 4
BREE

I jolt awake gasping. But I'm not in my bed.

I'm standing in the chamber of mirrors, bare feet cold against stone that's littered with ash. Gray dust swirls around my ankles with every shaky breath, and the air tastes metallic and old—like it remembers choices that turned to ruin.

This isn't right. The chamber was whole when I was here before. Ancient but intact.

Now the mirrors that line the walls are shattered, jagged edges reflecting nothing but broken darkness. Ash piles scattered across the floor where something once stood. Where someone once stood. The space feels hollow, gutted, like a place where hope came to die.

My heart hammers against my ribs. How did I get here? I was sleeping—Stellan's arm around me, his presence finally quieting the visions. I was safe.

I turn in a slow circle, trying to make sense of the destruction, and that's when I notice it.

One mirror remains intact.

It stands directly across from me, tall and elegant, its silver surface gleaming despite the ruin around it. And in that glass, I see myself—but not the me that's here, barefoot in ash and wearing a wrinkled sleep shirt.

This reflection stands in what looks like the same chamber, but whole. Beautiful. Light pools around her feet instead of dust, and the surfaces behind her glow with soft, ethereal radiance. She looks poised, confident, every gesture flowing with a grace I've never possessed.

She looks like a queen.

And she's looking right at me.

My reflection shouldn't be able to do that. Shouldn't be able to tilt her head and smile like she's been waiting. Like she knows something I don't.

I take a step toward the mirror, drawn by something I can't name. The ash crunches under my feet, but in the reflection, she moves across smooth stone that seems to shimmer with its own light.

When I'm close enough to touch the glass, I stop.

She raises her hand, pressing her palm against the surface from her side. Waiting.

I should walk away. Should find a way back to my bed, back to safety. But something in her expression—in my expression—makes me lift my own hand.

The moment my palm meets the glass, the world tilts.

Light explodes across my vision, silver and warm and impossibly bright. The sensation of falling—or flying—and then everything settles into a new kind of stillness.

I'm still in the chamber of mirrors, but everything has changed.

The air feels different here—lighter, charged with possibility instead of loss. The mirrors around me pulse with gentle radiance, their surfaces whole and clean. The floor beneath my feet is smooth pale stone that seems to hold its own inner glow, and delicate light drifts through the space like captured starlight.

It's breathtaking. Sacred. Perfect.

And across the chamber, she's waiting for me.

"Finally. You came."

Her voice carries easily across the space, calm and sure. She steps forward, and I watch myself move with a confidence I've never felt. This version of me belongs here, in this beautiful place. She looks at home among the light and the glow.

I look down at myself—still barefoot, still in my sleep shirt, but somehow the wrinkles have smoothed away. Even here, though, I feel small. Uncertain.

"Who are you?" The words come out smaller than I intended.

"You already know." She moves closer, each step deliberate and graceful. "I'm you. Without the chains."

"You don't feel like me."

"Because you've spent your whole life being smaller than you are." She stops just out of arm's reach, studying me with green eyes that hold no doubt, no fear. "Do you see it now? The difference between what is and what could be?"

I gesture helplessly at the glowing chamber around us. "This isn't real. Chambers don't just—"

"You're looking at the same place," she interrupts gently. "You see it as you believe yourself to be—broken, surrounded by the ashes of failed choices. I see it as it truly is." Her smile is soft but unyielding. "Sacred. Powerful. Beautiful."

The mist begins to curl around my feet, hesitant and uncertain. In this place, it looks almost apologetic—like it knows it doesn't belong among all this light.

She holds up her hands, and between her palms, something flows like liquid starlight. Not chaotic like my mist, but purposeful. Controlled. Beautiful.

"It hurts people," I whisper, staring at the wild, unpredictable thing that follows me everywhere.

"No." Her voice carries absolute certainty. "You're the one afraid of being worth their hurt."

"That's not—I didn't choose this." The words tumble out desperate and raw. "I didn't ask for the power, the bonds, the way everyone looks at me like I'm supposed to save them. I'm ruining everything."

"They've already chosen." She steps closer, and the light between her hands grows brighter. "You're the only one still refusing."

"Chosen what? To get hurt because of me? To have their lives turned upside down?"

"To love you." The words hit somewhere inside I didn't know existed. "To follow you. To build something new with you." Her expression softens with something that might be pity. "You think you're destroying them? No. You're what they've been waiting for."

I shake my head, backing away until I hit solid mirror. But this one doesn't shatter—it holds firm, reflecting my face back at me with startling clarity.

"I don't want this. I don't want to be responsible for—"

"For what? Their happiness? Their power? Their choice to stand with you?" She moves closer still, until I can see myself reflected in her eyes—but not the me that's here, uncertain and afraid. The me she sees is steady. Strong. Worthy.

"You call it ruin," she continues, voice carrying the weight of absolute truth. "I call it rebirth. You think this power is a curse. I've always known it's a gift."

The beautiful chamber seems to pulse around us, responding to her words. The light grows warmer, more welcoming, and for a moment I can almost feel what she feels—the rightness of power claimed instead of feared.

"A bond isn't a burden," she says softly. "It's loyalty sworn. Strength, not weight." She tilts her head, studying me. "Do you still believe you're too small for this?"

My knees buckle, and I slide down the mirror at my back until I'm sitting on the glowing floor. "I don't know how to be what they need."

"I lead because I never doubted I should." She kneels in front of me, close enough that I can see the certainty in her expression. "You'll be me, one way or another. The only choice is how long you fight it."

"I don't want to be you," I whisper.

She smiles then—gentle but implacable. "Then you don't want to be yourself."

The beautiful chamber starts to flicker around the edges, the light wavering like a candle in wind. My vision blurs as something pulls at me—the Ether backlash, too much power with nowhere to go.

"You're not weak," her voice echoes as everything begins to fade. "You're just afraid of how strong you truly are."

The last thing I see before the light takes me is her reaching out, as if to touch my face.

"When we become whole, you won't have to question being worthy of anything."

The words follow me as I fall backward through silver light, through the sensation of glass breaking and reforming, through the cold shock of reality rushing back in.

I wake on my bedroom floor, whole body shaking like I've been struck by lightning. The sanctuary's curved walls spin around me, silver script pulsing too bright, too fast.

Voices. Footsteps. The door slamming open.

"Bree!"

Someone drops to their knees beside me—Gray, his hands hovering like he wants to touch but doesn't know if it's safe. Behind him, the others crowd in the doorway: Rhett with heat radiating from his skin, Jace's knives already in his hands, Theo's eyes wide with Seer-panic.

Wes pushes through, falling to my other side. "What happened? You screamed—"

"I was there," I whisper, still tasting light on my tongue even though it doesn't make sense. "The chamber. But it was different. All ash and ruin, then—" I stop, not sure how to explain crossing through a mirror into a world that felt more real than real.

"Where?" Thane appears behind the others, silver eyes sharp with something that looks like recognition.

I struggle to sit up, my whole body still trembling with aftershock. Gray helps me, his hands steady and warm.

"Through the mirror," I manage. "To the other side. Where everything was beautiful. And she was there—" I stop, not sure how to describe meeting yourself and finding a stranger.

The silence stretches, heavy with questions none of us know how to ask.

I close my eyes, but I can still see her—confident, whole, looking at me like I'm the shadow and she's the light.

When I open them again, everyone's watching me with expressions I can't quite read.

"Riley," I whisper, the name slipping out before I can stop it.

Because somehow, impossibly, I know that's what she calls herself.

The silence that follows feels heavy, loaded with questions none of us know how to ask. But it's not the others' confusion that makes my skin prickle—it's the way Stellan goes completely still.

Not the casual stillness he usually wears like armor. This is different. Predatory. Like he's just heard something that changes everything.

When I look at him, his gray eyes are fixed on me with an intensity that makes me want to shrink back into the floor.

Like he's just seen a ghost step out of legend.

Chapter 5

STELLAN

The name hits me like a blade between the ribs.

Riley.

Not just the word itself, but the way Bree says it—with recognition, with certainty, like she's naming something that's always existed. Something that was waiting to be acknowledged.

I don't move from my position against the far wall, don't let so much as a flicker cross my expression. But inside, everything goes cold and sharp and hungry.

It shouldn't be possible. The Ashen Oath died with the last of the mirror queens three centuries ago. Nothing more than whispers passed around fire-lit halls, stories Feeders told each other in the dark spaces between hunger and satisfaction. And my own curiosity.

Yet Bree just named her. And my body knows the truth before my mind can cage it.

The others cluster around her like moths drawn to flame—Gray's steady hands helping her sit up, Wes hovering close enough to catch her if she falls again, Rhett radiating protective heat from the doorway. Even Theo leans forward, Seer's eyes trying to pierce whatever veil she's just crossed through. Zira watches from the corner, uncharacteristically quiet, arms crossed like she's cataloging every word.

They move toward her instinctively, and the Ether responds, curling silver threads between them like loyalty already sworn. Like bonds recognized and claimed.

I stay perfectly still. Predators don't crowd their prey—not when the prey might bolt, and certainly not when other hunters are circling.

Instead, I watch. And I think.

The legends speak of a chamber lined with mirrors, where the chosen stood before themselves unbroken. Where an oath was made not with words alone, but by becoming whole—two halves of a soul joining across the space between what is and what could be.

The stories always hinged on the name. The mirror self had to be named, acknowledged, claimed. Only then could the Oath begin.

For centuries, we treated it as fairy tale. Hope dressed as mythology, told by those who'd forgotten what it meant to be complete. Even among Feeders, who understand hunger and incompleteness better than most, the Ashen Oath was bedtime fantasy.

But I've just watched it happen.

Bree didn't dream. She didn't hallucinate or break under pressure. She touched the core of something that was supposed to be extinct.

"She was so sure," Bree whispers, and her voice carries that particular quality of someone who's seen truth and found it terrifying. "Like she'd been waiting for me. Like she already knew how everything would end."

Thane shifts closer, silver eyes calculating. He's thinking tactically—how this affects his position, his mission, the Council's interests. Useful, but limited. He sees politics where he should see prophecy.

"What did she look like?" Gray asks gently, and I can hear the effort it takes him to keep his voice steady.

"Like me. But..." Bree struggles for words, gesturing helplessly. "Whole. Like she'd never questioned whether she deserved to exist. She stood in this beautiful place, all light and mirrors, and I was—" She stops, pressing her palms against her eyes. "I was standing in ash."

The imagery sends something cold sliding down my spine. Two chambers. Two versions of the same truth, experienced through two different lenses of self-worth.

That's when I know for certain. This isn't just Ether manifestation or magical bleeding between realms. This is the Ashen Oath awakening, piece by piece, choice by choice. And if the Oath is real, if it's happening, then Bree isn't just Scarborne nobility returned from exile. She isn't just an inconvenient magical surge for the Council to contain.

She's the hinge point. The one whose choice will reshape everything.

And I want to be there when she makes it.

"Did she say anything else?" Wes asks, voice carefully controlled. But I can taste the hunger coming off him too, different from mine but just as sharp. The awakening Incubus in him recognizes what the rest haven't yet grasped—that Bree's power is evolving, deepening, becoming something none of us anticipated.

"She said I'd be her eventually." Bree's laugh holds no humor. "That the only choice was how long I'd fight it."

There. The prophecy, spoken in her own words.

I glance at Thane and find him watching me with that peculiar intensity of his. We're rivals by nature—vampire and incubus, both predators, both drawn to the same impossible girl. But we're also the only ones in this room who understand what she's just described.

The others see fragments. Confusion. Something to be solved or protected against.

We see the moment everything changed.

Bree shivers, pulling what looks like Rhett's hoodie tighter around herself. The gesture is small, vulnerable, utterly human. It doesn't match the cosmic weight of what she's just experienced, and somehow that makes it more unsettling.

She thinks she's fractured. Thinks she's failing them all by not being ready for power that chose her before she was born.

But I've just seen the proof—she's the hinge. The Oath lives in her, waits in her, grows stronger every time she doubts herself into that chamber of ash and ruin.

"It felt so real," she whispers.

"Because it was," I say quietly, speaking for the first time since her revelation.

Every head turns toward me. Bree's green eyes are wide, still shocked, but there's something else there now. Recognition, maybe. Or fear.

"You know what this is," Thane says. Not a question.

I push off from the wall with deliberate grace, taking a single step closer to their circle. Close enough to be part of the conversation, but not so close that I crowd her.

"I know the stories," I say carefully. "The old ones. The ones most assume are myth."

"Tell us," Gray says, voice carrying that note of command he probably doesn't realize he's using.

Something in me responds to the authority in his tone before I can stop it. Interesting.

I meet Bree's eyes instead of his. Because this isn't about what they need to know. It's about what she's ready to hear.

"The Ashen Oath," I say simply.

Just the name is enough to still the air.

"What does that mean?" Gray demands.

I let silence stretch, then glance at Bree. Her green eyes are wide, still shocked, but there's recognition there now. Fear, maybe. Or understanding.

"It means the stories weren't just stories," I say quietly.

Jace bristles. "And?"

My smile is small, sharp. "And that's all you get tonight."

I let the silence settle, then step into it. Not close enough to touch her. Just close enough they all feel the weight of what I'm not saying.

From the corner, I catch Zira watching me instead of Bree. Her dark eyes are calculating, filing away my reaction for later examination. She notices everything.

"The rest," I say, letting my gaze settle on Bree, "depends on her."

And I'll be there when she decides.

Chapter 6
THEO

Two days of questions that no one will answer.

Two days of watching Bree avoid eye contact whenever I'm in the room, like she's afraid I'll see too much again. Like what happened in that mirror realm scared her enough that keeping distance feels safer than letting me close.

I tried to apologize yesterday. Cornered her in the hallway outside her room, words tumbling out about how sorry I was for what happened at the end—for pushing when she needed space, for letting my vision overwhelm the moment when she was already drowning. She just looked at me with those green eyes gone carefully blank and said, *"It's fine, Theo. Really."*

But it's not fine. The way she barely lets our eyes meet now, the careful distance she maintains even when we're in the same room—none of it is fine. And I can't shake the feeling that I broke something fragile between us when I let my Seer instincts override my common sense.

Two days of Stellan's elegant dismissals and Thane's cold refusals every time I try to understand what the Ashen Oath actually means.

And two days of visions that make no sense.

Not about Bree this time. About Seth.

I see him standing beside two figures—Phil, and with him, a man whose face shifts every time I try to focus on it, something infinitely more predatory lurking beneath the surface. They're talking in low voices, planning something. But then the vision fractures, and I see Seth again—standing between Bree and danger, protective, chosen, *belonging*. Two futures flickering like competing flames.

The contradiction gnaws at me. Seth working with someone who wants to hurt her, but also Seth saving her. Seth betraying everything we've built, but also Seth earning his place among us.

Both futures feel equally real. Equally possible.

It makes me want to scream.

"Not everything is for you to know, Seer," Stellan said yesterday, voice smooth as silk and twice as cutting. When I pressed, his smile went sharp. *"Some knowledge is earned, not given."*

Thane was more direct. *"Ask again, and you'll regret it."*

So I stopped asking them.

Instead, I turned to what I do best: quiet obsession.

The sanctuary has a small library tucked into one of the restored wings—shelves of books that appeared the same way everything else here does, in response to need and intention. Most are general magical theory, histories of the various factions, treatises on Ether manipulation that make my head spin.

But scattered through them are fragments. Mentions of mirror rites and oaths sworn between selves. References to chambers where choice became destiny. Never enough to understand, always enough to frustrate.

The name *Riley* appears nowhere. Not once.

But *Ashen* does. *Oath* does. Always fractured, always incomplete, like someone tried to erase the knowledge but couldn't quite manage it.

After sixteen hours of reading, my eyes burn and my hands shake with the effort of not throwing the books across the room. I need air. I need space. I need to move before I shatter something.

The sanctuary grounds stretch beyond the main building in ways that seem to shift depending on who's exploring them. When Bree walks the paths, flowers bloom and trees bend toward her like she's the sun. When Rhett trains outside, the fire-resistant stones arrange themselves into perfect practice rings.

When I walk them now, frustrated and hungry for answers, they lead me deeper than I've ever gone.

Past the garden, training areas and the meditation circles. Into sections where the paths become older, more overgrown, like they haven't been walked in decades.

Something hums faintly under my skin—not a vision, but something close. A whisper of recognition, of rightness, pulling me forward even though I don't understand why.

That's when I hear footsteps behind me.

I turn, expecting Rhett or maybe Gray checking on me, but it's Seth who emerges from the tree line. His sandy hair is disheveled, shirt sleeves pushed up like he's been working, and there's something careful in his expression. Cautious.

"Hey," he says, stopping a few feet away. Like he's not sure he's welcome.

"Seth." I nod, not moving closer or farther. "You're pretty far from the main buildings."

"So are you." He shoves his hands into his pockets, shoulders hunching slightly. "Look, I... I wanted to apologize. For the other night. When you had that vision and came running out—" He stops, jaw working. "I know how it must have looked. Me being alone with her in the garden. I wasn't trying to... I mean, I wouldn't—" He trails off, looking uncomfortable.

I study his face, looking for any trace of the threat I saw in my vision. But all I see is genuine regret and something that looks like confusion.

"I was protecting her," I say simply. "Or trying to. The vision felt so real."

"I know. And I get it. But..." Seth runs a hand through his hair. "She looked at me like she didn't know if she could trust me after that. Like maybe your vision was right and there really is something wrong with me."

There's something vulnerable in his voice that catches me off guard.

Seth falls into step beside me as I start walking again, and for a while we don't talk. Just move through dappled sunlight and the whisper of leaves overhead. It's easier than I expected—his presence somehow familiar despite how recently he joined us.

"She's avoiding me now," he says eventually. "Bree. I don't blame her, but..." He trails off, shaking his head. "I don't want her to hate me. And I don't know how not to screw this up. Not when she has all of you."

He kicks at a loose stone on the path. "I heard someone in town call you guys the *Ether Entourage*—like you're this... unit. And I'm just some random guy who showed up and complicated everything." His voice drops lower, more bitter. "But I can't help it. There's something about her that... I feel drawn to her. Like I'm supposed to be here. And I know that probably sounds crazy, but—"

The words hit something raw in my chest. Because I've seen it—the screwing up, the betrayal, the way his choices could tear everything apart. But I've also seen the other path, the one where he stands with us instead of against us.

"You know," I say quietly, not looking at him, "you don't have to be whole to be worthy of being seen. Not by her. Not by anyone."

Seth goes completely still beside me. When I glance over, there's something vulnerable and stunned in his expression, like I've just said something he's never let himself believe. The same words I uttered to Bree all those years ago the first time, are just as true for him.

For a long moment, he doesn't speak. Just stares at the path ahead, jaw working like he's trying to find words that won't crack his voice.

"I..." he starts, then stops. Clears his throat. "That's not—I mean, how do you know that?" The question comes out rougher than he probably intended. "About being broken. About her not... not caring about that."

There's something desperate in his voice, like he's asking for permission to hope.

"Because I've seen the way she looks at all of us," I say softly. "The way she chose to let us stay, even when she was terrified. She doesn't need us to be perfect, Seth. She just needs us to be real."

He nods slowly, but I can see him struggling with it. Wanting to believe but not quite daring to.

"You're not the only one who feels that way," I add, even softer.

We walk in comfortable silence after that, the path winding deeper into sections of the sanctuary I've never explored. Ancient oak trees with trunks wide enough to hide behind. Stone markers half-buried in ivy. The sense of old magic sleeping in the very soil.

"You're looking for something," Seth observes after we've been walking for ten minutes. "Not just walking off frustration."

I glance at him, surprised by his perceptiveness. "What makes you say that?"

"The way you keep scanning. Like you're following a trail only you can see." He pauses, considering. "If I were hiding something, I'd probably leave a marker where no one would notice."

"And where would that be?"

Seth stops walking, head tilted like he's listening to something. When he looks at me, there's an odd intensity in his eyes. "Somewhere that looks forgotten but isn't. Somewhere that feels empty but holds memory."

The words hit something in my chest. Recognition. Like he's just voiced what my visions have been trying to tell me.

I close my eyes, letting the whisper-pull strengthen. When I open them, Seth is watching me with curious attention but no judgment.

"This way," I say, turning left toward what looks like a dead end in the trees.

But as we push through the undergrowth, it opens into a clearing I know wasn't here yesterday. Or maybe it was, and we just weren't ready to find it.

In the center stands the ruins of what might have been a small temple. Crumbling stone walls barely waist-high, covered in moss and threading vines. But carved into every visible surface are symbols—spirals and curves that hurt to look at directly, like they're moving just outside the edge of vision.

And scattered among the ruins, catching light that shouldn't exist in the shadow of the trees, are pieces of broken mirror.

"Well," Seth says quietly. "That's not ominous at all."

I step closer, drawn by the same instinct that led us here. When I kneel beside one of the larger mirror shards, I can see why.

The reflection it shows isn't quite right. Not distorted, but... layered. Like there's something else behind the surface, watching.

"Theo." Seth's voice carries a warning. "Maybe don't—"

But I'm already reaching out, fingertips brushing the edge of the mirror shard.

It ripples.

Not violently like when Bree's power surges, but gently. Like recognition. Like greeting an old friend.

For just a moment, I see it—the chamber as it used to be. Whole mirrors lining intact walls. Figures standing before their reflections, hands pressed to glass, choices being made that shaped the magical world.

And then, layered beneath that vision like an echo: Seth again. Standing in this very clearing, but changed. Older. Marked by choices not yet made. Behind him, the shadow of the man with the shifting face. Before him, Bree's hand outstretched, offering forgiveness he doesn't think he deserves.

Both futures. Both real. Both waiting for him to choose.

Then the vision fades, but something else begins.

The ground beneath us starts to shift.

Not violently—more like breathing. Like the earth itself is exhaling after holding its breath for centuries. Seth stumbles backward as stones roll away from beneath our feet, and I scramble up from where I'm kneeling.

"Theo, what did you—"

But his words are cut off as the center of the ruined temple sinks inward, revealing what was hidden beneath. Stone steps, worn smooth by age, spiraling down into darkness. The mirror shards scattered across the ruins begin to catch light that doesn't exist, reflecting something that isn't there.

The air that drifts up from below smells ancient—not stale, but old in the way that sacred places feel old. Like incense and time and choices that echo through centuries. But underneath it, something else. Something that tastes like copper and hunger, like the space between breaths when you're not sure if you'll be allowed another.

"It recognizes you," Seth says quietly, staring at the entrance that wasn't there moments before. His voice carries an odd note, almost like relief mixed with fear. "Because you're one of hers."

I look at him, surprised by his certainty.

"The way you touched the mirror," he explains, voice hushed with awe. "The way the ground responded. This place knows you belong to her."

The words hit something deep in my chest. Something that's been aching since Bree started avoiding my eyes, since she looked at me with that careful blankness and said *"It's fine, Theo. Really."*

Maybe it's not fine between us right now. Maybe I did push too hard, overwhelm her when she was already drowning. But this—this ancient place recognizing me, responding to my touch because I'm hers—it means something. It means the connection between us isn't broken, just... strained.

The pull I've been feeling all day intensifies, drawing me toward those spiral steps like a compass needle finding true north. But Seth's right—we can't go down there unprepared. And something about the air rising from below makes my skin crawl, like whatever waits in the darkness has been patient for too long.

"We need light," I say, though every instinct screams at me to descend immediately. "And we need to tell the others."

Seth nods, but he's studying the opening with that same intensity I've been feeling. "This is it, isn't it? The real chamber. Where the Ashen Oath actually happens."

"I think so." I can barely tear my gaze away from the entrance. "But I also think Bree needs to be the one to go down first."

"Because it's hers."

"Because she's the only one who can make the choice." I look at him, weighing my words carefully. Thinking about those two futures I keep seeing, the way they flicker like competing flames. "I think you should be there too. When we tell them. When we come back."

Seth goes completely still. "You do?"

"You found this place with me. You helped make it possible." I pause, watching his expression. "And I think... I think she'll need all of us. Whatever choice she has to make down there."

Something shifts in his face—surprise, maybe hope, maybe fear. Like he's hearing an invitation he didn't expect and isn't sure he deserves.

I think about the vision again. Seth standing between Bree and danger. Seth offering protection instead of betrayal. The path where he chooses to stand with us instead of against us.

"I think you get to decide that," I say. "But yes. I think you belong here."

We stand there for a long moment, staring at the entrance to something that's been waiting beneath the sanctuary grounds for who knows how long. Waiting for her. Waiting for this moment.

"You felt that," Seth says finally. Not a question.

I nod, the mirror shard pulsing warm against my ribs—like a heartbeat, like recognition, like acknowledgment of what we've found.

"This changes everything," Seth says quietly. "She'll want to know."

"She needs to know." The words come out with more certainty than I've felt in days. "Whatever the others have been protecting her from, whatever they think she's not ready for—this is hers to decide."

Seth nods. "So we tell her."

"We tell her." I look back toward the sanctuary, toward where Bree is probably still avoiding my eyes, still keeping that careful distance. "And maybe... maybe this will help fix what I broke between us."

The mirror shard continues to pulse against my skin as we walk back toward the sanctuary, its rhythm matching my heartbeat. The feeling spreads through my chest, certain and grounding—like I'm finally carrying something that matters.

"I'll tell her," I say, the words coming easier now. "Tonight. No more waiting for permission from people who think they know what's best for her."

"And then?"

I think about Bree's careful distance, the way she's been avoiding my eyes since the mirror realm. About how much I want things to go back to the way they were between us. But that's not what this is about.

"And then she gets to choose what comes next," I say quietly. "Even if that choice doesn't include me. Even if she never forgives me for pushing too hard in the mirror realm."

The words hurt to say, but they're true. Whatever waits in that chamber below, whatever the Ashen Oath truly means—it's hers to discover. Her choice to make.

And if bringing her this discovery is the last thing I ever do for her, if it costs me whatever chance I had of earning her trust back—it's still the right thing to do.

Because loving someone means wanting what's best for them, even when it breaks your heart.

The words come out sharper than I intended, edged with frustration and longing and the kind of desperate hope I usually keep buried. Seth doesn't flinch, but something flickers across his expression.

Understanding, maybe. Or recognition of his own hunger to matter, to be chosen, to be seen as essential rather than expendable.

We walk back toward the sanctuary in silence, but it's different now. Weighted with shared discovery and the knowledge that we're both carrying pieces of something larger than ourselves.

I still don't know which Seth this is—the one who'll stand with us, or the one who'll tear everything apart. The visions flicker between both futures like competing flames, and only his choices will determine which one comes to pass. But for now, in this moment, he feels like an ally.

Maybe that's enough for today.

The mirror shard pulses steadily against my skin, a reminder of what we've found. What Bree needs to know.

Whatever comes next, whatever choice she has to make—at least she'll have all the pieces. At least no one will be able to keep the truth from her anymore.

Even me.

Chapter 7
Jace

Sleep is for people who don't have thoughts ricocheting around their skull like pinballs at three in the morning.

I've been staring at the ceiling for two hours, listening to the sanctuary's quiet hum and trying not to think about everything that's been building tension in this place lately. Theo's weird visions. Bree avoiding everyone like we've all got the plague. The way Thane showed up and suddenly the air tastes different—sharper, more electric.

And then there's whatever's been happening with Wes.

He's been... different. More awake somehow, like he's been sleepwalking for years and only just noticed. The way he looks at people now, like he's seeing layers beneath the surface. It should be unsettling.

It is unsettling.

But not in a bad way, which is maybe the most unsettling part of all.

I roll out of bed with a frustrated sigh. When my brain won't shut up, there's only one solution: make something that requires just enough focus to drown out the noise but not so much that I actually have to think.

Pancakes.

Perfect chaos food. Flour, eggs, milk, heat—simple enough that even I can't screw it up too badly. And if I'm being honest, there's a tiny part of me that wants to show up Mairen. Sweet woman, incredible cook, but she's been making breakfast for everyone like it's her personal mission to feed the entire magical world.

Time to prove that the sanctuary's resident knife-throwing disaster can handle a skillet without setting anything on fire.

Pancake supremacy, here I come.

The kitchen is dark when I pad down the hallway, bare feet silent on cool stone. One of the many perks of growing up learning to move without sound—midnight snack raids become an art form.

I flip on just enough lights to see what I'm doing, then make a beeline for the massive pantry. The sanctuary's version of food storage is about as subtle as everything else here—carved wooden doors that could double as castle gates, shelves that stretch up toward a vaulted ceiling, enough supplies to feed an army.

Or a bunch of magically awakening twenty-somethings with supernatural metabolisms.

I'm already mentally cataloging what I need—flour, baking powder, maybe some vanilla if this place runs fancy—when I swing open the pantry door.

And stop dead.

What the hell—

Wes and Gray are inside.

Not just standing close. Not just having a conversation.

Making out.

Gray's back is pressed against the far wall, Wes's hands braced on either side of his head, and they're kissing like the world might end if they stop. Wes's dark curls are messed up from Gray's fingers, and Gray's usual careful control is completely gone, replaced by something raw and hungry that makes my breath catch.

I just stand there. Staring. Like my brain has completely forgotten how to process what my eyes are seeing.

We all freeze at exactly the same moment.

Three pairs of eyes. Complete silence except for the sound of someone's ragged breathing—might be mine.

I slam the door shut.

Stand there in the hallway like an idiot, heart hammering against my ribs.

Nope. Nope nope nope. Did not see that. Definitely did not see Gray looking like that. Definitely did not notice the way Wes—

I crack the door open again.

They're both still there.

Because really—where the hell would they go?

And now they're staring at me. Gray's face is flushed, lips slightly swollen, looking guilty but also... not. Like he's been caught but isn't particularly sorry about it.

Wes just looks amused.

I take a deep breath—trying to look like I'm just getting my bearings and not like I'm drowning in whatever the hell this feeling is—and push the door open wider.

"Uh." The word comes out like I've forgotten how language works. "Don't mind me. Just... pancakes."

Of course the flour is right there on the shelf. Right between them. Because the universe apparently has a sense of humor and it's terrible.

"The flour is…" I gesture vaguely, hoping one of them will just grab it and toss it to me so I can disappear back to the kitchen and pretend this never happened.

Instead, Wes steps back just enough to clear a path, and the smile that curves his lips is pure trouble. Like he can see right through my casual deflection to whatever is churning underneath.

"Go ahead," Wes says, voice low and still slightly breathless. "We're not stopping you."

I have to step into the pantry. Have to reach between their bodies, close enough to catch the heat radiating off Gray's skin, close enough to see the way Wes's pupils are dilated in the dim light.

My fingers hover for just a second—this is inevitable, but that doesn't make it easier—before I grab the flour. The brush against Gray's arm as I pull back is soft, brief, electric.

Gray inhales sharply. When I glance up, Wes is watching me with something that looks almost like recognition. Like he knows exactly what that accidental contact did to my pulse.

"Sorry," I mutter, backing toward the door with the flour clutched against my chest like armor. "Didn't mean to… interrupt."

"You didn't," Gray says quietly, but there's something in his voice I can't quite identify.

Wes doesn't say anything. Just watches me retreat with that small, knowing smile that makes my stomach flip in ways I don't want to think about right now. Maybe ever.

I escape back to the kitchen and immediately throw myself into mixing batter with way more enthusiasm than the task requires. Whisk clattering against the bowl, measuring cups banging against the counter—anything to make enough noise to drown out the replay loop my brain seems determined to run.

It's fine. Totally fine. So what if Gray and Wes are... whatever that was. So what if Gray's hands were in Wes's hair and Wes was looking at him like he wanted to devour him whole. So what if they both looked at me like—

Nope. Not going there.

I focus on the batter. Flour, eggs, milk, a splash of vanilla. Simple. Straightforward. Nothing complicated about pancakes. Nothing emotional. Just flour, eggs, milk. Breakfast, not a breakdown. Nothing that requires me to think about the way Gray's shoulders looked pressed against that wall, or the sound Wes made when I brushed past him, or the fact that I apparently have opinions about both of those things.

When did that happen?

The whisk moves faster. Probably too fast. I'm definitely overmixing, but stopping means thinking, and thinking is not on the agenda right now.

I don't hear the pantry door open again. Don't hear footsteps on the kitchen floor.

The first sign I'm not alone anymore is the heat against my back—body warmth close enough to feel but not quite touching.

Then Wes's voice, low and intimate, right by my ear:

"Your secret's safe with me."

I freeze, knuckles going white around the whisk handle. Every muscle in my body locks up like I've been struck by lightning.

"What secret?" I manage, trying for casual and missing by about a mile.

"The one you *liked*."

The words hit somewhere deep inside, sending heat racing through my veins and making my pulse stutter. I want to spin around, want to face him, want to demand what the hell he thinks he's talking about.

Instead, I stay perfectly still, staring down at the batter like it holds the secrets of the universe.

"I don't know what you mean," I say, and even I don't believe it.

Wes chuckles, soft and knowing. "Sure you don't."

When I finally work up the nerve to turn around, he's already walking away. Casual as anything, like he didn't just turn my entire world sideways with a handful of words.

He pauses in the doorway, glances back over his shoulder.

"For what it's worth," he says, "Gray's a good kisser. But I think you already figured that out."

And then he's gone, leaving me standing there with half-mixed batter and a heart that's beating so fast I'm surprised it doesn't crack a rib.

I stare at the bowl, trying to process what just happened. Trying to figure out what the hell Wes thinks he saw, what he thinks he knows about me.

Trying to figure out why the idea of Gray being a good kisser makes something tight and hungry unfurl in my chest.

The batter is definitely overmixed now. Probably ruined. But I keep whisking anyway, because stopping means admitting that everything just changed, and I'm not ready for that.

I'm not ready to think about Gray. Or Wes. Or the way they both looked at me like they could see straight through every wall I've ever built.

The pancakes are going to burn, and it won't be the batter's fault.

Chapter 8
BREE

The kitchen smells like a crime scene.

Burnt flour. Something that might have been pancakes in another life-time. The kind of disaster that requires actual scraping to remove from cookware.

I'm standing in the wreckage, holding what I think used to be breakfast, when footsteps approach behind me.

But my mind keeps drifting to last night. To Stellan appearing in my doorway like he'd been summoned by my restlessness, slipping into bed behind me with that quiet question: *"Okay?"*

I'd fallen asleep in his arms. Actually slept, deep and dreamless, for the first time in days. But when I woke up this morning, I was alone, and there was this hollow feeling in my chest that I don't know how to name.

What did it mean? And why did part of me wish he'd still been there?

"Well," Zira says, appearing in the doorway. "Someone had a morning."

"Jace tried to cook." I drop the pancake-shaped brick back onto the plate with a thunk. "Emphasis on tried."

She surveys the carnage - flour coating every surface, a mixing bowl abandoned in the sink, what looks like egg shells scattered across the counter. "What happened? Did he forget how fire works?"

"He was distracted."

Zira's eyebrow quirks. "Distracted how?"

I shrug. "I don't know. He just seemed... off this morning. Flustered."

She starts moving through the kitchen, collecting destroyed dishes with practiced efficiency. There's something easy about the way she works, like she's done this before - cleaned up someone else's emotional disasters.

"You know," she says, scraping carbon off a pan, "in my experience, men only cook this badly when they're thinking about something else. Something that's got them all turned around."

The way she says it makes me look at her more closely. "Speaking from experience?"

Her smile is sharp and knowing. "Oh, honey. I've seen this exact mess before."

We work in comfortable silence for a few minutes. It's nice, having another woman here who doesn't expect me to explain or justify or perform. She just... helps.

"So," she says, rinsing a bowl. "Thane seems... different this morning."

My hands still on the dish I'm drying. "Different how?"

"Less like he's about to murder someone. More like..." She pauses, studying my face. "Like he found something he wasn't expecting to find."

Heat crawls up my throat. I keep my eyes on the plate, scrubbing at a spot that isn't there.

"Bree." Her voice softens, but there's steel underneath. "What happened?"

"Nothing," I say too quickly. "It's—"

"Don't lie to me." Her eyes sharpen. "I can feel it on you."

My stomach flips. The cloth slips from my hands. "We... we bonded. A couple days ago."

Zira goes completely still. When I finally look up, she's staring at me like I just told her I'd rewritten the laws of magic.

"Was he feeding when it happened?"

My face burns. "Yes."

"Gods." She sets down the bowl with shaking hands. "Bree, do you understand what you've done?"

"I—"

"You bonded with the Council's Feeder representative. The highest-ranking Feeder in the magical world." Her voice drops to a whisper. "I told you. You're changing everything."

"What do you mean?"

"Feeding bonds are possessive. If he tries to feed elsewhere without your permission, it'll feel empty. Wrong." She studies my face. "But more than that—you just made a statement to every Feeder alive. The Source accepts us. Chooses us. Bonds with us."

My chest tightens. "I didn't think—"

"No, you didn't think. You just acted on instinct and heart." Her expression shifts, something like awe creeping in. "And that's exactly what they needed to see."

Before I can respond, a sound cuts through the air outside. Not voices—a hum. Low and resonant, like hundreds of people breathing in unison.

Zira's posture shifts instantly. The easy domesticity disappears, replaced by something sharp and alert. But there's no fear in her expression. Instead, something like anticipation flickers across her face.

"What is that?" I ask.

She moves to the window and peers out, going very still for a long moment.

"Three hundred," she says quietly, stepping back from the glass. "Maybe more. And this is just the beginning."

My blood turns to ice. "Three hundred what?"

"Feeders. Here for you."

The words make my head spin. Three hundred. Here for me.

"Bree!" Gray's voice now, closer. Urgent but not panicked. "You need to see this!"

The mist explodes around me, wild and protective, responding to the spike of adrenaline shooting through my chest.

Zira just watches it all with that same knowing expression, her smirk widening.

"I told you, Bree," she says, voice rich with satisfaction. "You're going to change everything."

Chapter 9
BREE

Three hundred Feeders kneel in the clearing beyond the sanctuary doors.

The thunder of three hundred knees striking earth still echoes through the sanctuary walls.

Now they wait in perfect silence, bodies pressed close enough that I can feel their collective breath, their hope, their desperation.

I hover just inside the threshold, close enough to see them but not committed to stepping out. My hand grips the doorframe, knuckles white.

Behind me, the guys cluster in the entry hall. Each one processing this differently.

Rhett paces, heat radiating off him in waves. All of his protective energy with nowhere to go.

Wes stands perfectly still, but his eyes are hungry. All those people—he can feel the pull. Except he's looking at me.

Gray leans against the wall, arms crossed, watching Wes and me more than the crowd. Waiting.

Jace spins a blade between his fingers, nervous energy crackling around him like static.

Theo sits on the bottom step, elbows on his knees, staring at nothing with that distant look that means he's seeing too much.

Stellan and Thane talking in hushed tones as if I might be spooked by whatever they'll say.

"This is getting ridiculous," I mumble, not annoyed but a little overwhelmed by the surreal nature of it all. Three hundred people. Kneeling. Again. They really need to stop that. "Anyone know when the sanctuary will be throwing up the 'no vacancy' sign?"

I hear Stellan shift behind me, his voice carrying a note of amusement. "That depends."

Thane clears his throat from closer than he was a moment ago. When did he move?

I glance at him, and he's looking right back at me now instead of at the crowd. Something shifts in his expression—softer than usual.

"It won't," he says quietly, silver eyes holding mine. "The sanctuary will expand and adjust, as long as your heart wills it."

The words settle somewhere under my ribs. Not just about the sanctuary. About him. About this.

About Us.

Stellan moves closer, his voice carrying that familiar note of calculated certainty. "Step with her, Thane. Let them see. They're waiting."

Right. Three hundred people. Still kneeling.

I take a breath and step forward.

My fingers find his sleeve without conscious thought, gripping the dark fabric. "With me," I whisper.

He glances down at where I'm holding onto him, and the smallest smirk graces his full lips. His hand covers mine, slides it down from his sleeve, and laces our fingers together. The warmth of his skin, the deliberate certainty of the gesture, sends a shiver through me.

When I look back into his silver eyes, the mask slips, just for a heartbeat, and I catch a glimpse of something raw underneath that makes my chest ache.

He nods.

We step forward together.

The Ether responds immediately—not to my fear this time, but to the bond humming between us. The silver mist rises, curling around our joined hands, threading between our fingers like liquid starlight.

And then it happens.

The bond connecting us now becomes visible—bright, undeniable, hanging in the air between Thane and me like a bridge made of pure light. It hums, alive, in rhythm with my heartbeat, then settles into a steady glow that every single Feeder in the clearing can see.

A gasp moves through them like a wave, three hundred voices breathing in at once.

The murmurs start immediately.

"Gods above," someone breathes.

"Is that—?"

"The bond. It's visible."

"I've never seen anything like it."

A woman near the front of the crowd rises to her feet, not aggressive but desperate for answers. Her voice carries over the rising whispers. "What does this mean? Does the Council sanction this union?"

More voices join hers, some reverent, others edged with panic.

"Is everything changing now?"

"What happens to the rest of us?"

"Are we free?"

And then, barely above a whisper from someone in the back:

"She chose him."

The words hit me in the chest, different from all the others. More personal. More true.

The questions pile on top of each other until the clearing buzzes with desperate hope and barely contained fear. I can feel their stares on me, measuring my every breath, tracking every flicker of expression.

They want answers I don't have. Promises I don't know if I can keep.

I open my mouth to say something—anything that might calm the rising tension—but my throat closes up. What if I say the wrong thing? What if I make a promise I can't fulfill, or give them hope I can't deliver on?

The silver strand pulses brighter, responding to the storm I can't contain.

Thane's hand squeezes mine—cool, steady, a contrast to the heat rushing under my skin. The touch grounds me, and for a moment the overwhelming weight of their expectations feels almost manageable.

"Whatever you choose to say," he murmurs, too low for the crowd to hear, "it will be the right thing."

The words make the ache in my chest grow. For a man who doesn't know me—not really—he seems to understand more than I want to admit.

I'm about to test his theory on words when something makes me scan the crowd.

Seth is halfway back, kneeling with the others, but his head is tilted up. Following his line of sight, I spot it—a black shape perched motionless in the mira tree above us.

A crow.

My stomach drops as Thane's words from that first day echo in my memory: *"Shifter. Council representative. Nyx."*

When I look back at Seth, the dread on his face confirms what I already know.

This isn't just a bird.

A rush of black wings cuts through the murmurs like a blade. The crowd breaks like a flock startled to flight, instinct bowing them even before the crow touched the ground.

Fear. Pure, instinctive fear.

A shadow drops from the sky, landing between me and the crowd with more grace than should be possible.

Feathers dissolve into flesh mid-fall. Black hair, sharp cheekbones, eyes that gleam with too much intelligence to be fully human.

Nyx.

This can't be good.

She straightens slowly, brushing imaginary dust from her dark clothes, and the easy smile curving her lips makes my stomach drop. This isn't someone who just happened to be in the neighborhood.

She doesn't bow. Doesn't kneel. Doesn't show even the pretense of respect.

Instead, she tilts her head at Thane, gaze flicking between the silver strand still glowing between us and his carefully controlled expression.

Her smile widens into something sharp and knowing.

"Tsk, tsk," she purrs, voice slicing through the stunned silence like a blade. "Now, Thane... you *know* better."

Chapter 10
STELLAN

I lounge against the sanctuary doorframe like I have all the time in the world and watch the show unfold.

While the others bristle—Rhett's heat spiking, Gray's shoulders rolling as something wild flickers behind his eyes, Jace going perfectly still in that dangerous way of his—I find myself genuinely entertained.

Nyx has always been theatrical. But there's an art to the way she commands a space, the way three hundred Feeders instinctively cower without her saying a word. She doesn't need to raise her voice. Her presence alone is enough to remind everyone exactly who holds the leash.

She doesn't bow. Doesn't even acknowledge the Source at Thane's side.

Instead, she focuses on Thane with the kind of disappointed smile that suggests intimate knowledge.

"Oh, Thane," she purrs, circling him like a predator savoring wounded prey. "Look at you. All that control, all that discipline—and for what?"

The silver strand still glows between him and Bree, impossible to ignore. Nyx's gaze follows it with something that might be amusement if it weren't so cold.

"After everything," she continues, voice dropping to something almost intimate. "After all of our interludes, our... *exploration*. How quick you forget where you used to spend your nights." She pauses, letting that sink in. "You choose to bind yourself to her?"

Bree goes rigid beside Thane. I catch the exact moment doubt creeps across her face—not jealousy, though there's that too. Something deeper. A question about what exactly Thane's relationship with the Council entails.

Thane's mask never slips, but his jaw ticks. "I serve where I'm needed."

"Do you?" Nyx's smile sharpens. "Because from where I'm standing, it looks like you've tied yourself into the Oath already. The strand won't save you when they come for her, you know."

The words hit me like ice water.

Tied into the Oath.

Not just bonded—*tied into the Oath.* That isn't language you use unless you've seen it before. Information like that is meat dropped in a pit of wolves. But how would she know about that unless—

Unless the Council knows more than they're letting on.

I file the information away, force my expression to remain bored. But every instinct I have is suddenly screaming that Nyx just revealed far more than she intended.

"The Council grows impatient," she says, turning her attention to Bree for the first time. Her tone shifts—still predatory, but with a mock-welcoming warmth that makes my skin crawl. "Especially now, with this bond on such public display."

She gestures to the crowd of still-kneeling Feeders, most of whom are trying to make themselves as small as possible.

"But don't worry, dear," Nyx continues, that razor smile widening. "An old friend is on his way to greet you. Someone who's been watching you for quite some time. He'll be so pleased to finally make proper introductions."

My blood goes cold. Only one name fits her little riddle, and it's the one I've been waiting to hear.

The others filled Thane and me in on everything that happened—the years of manipulation, the advances, even the cameras. Everything that led up to Bree broken on her apartment floor. Besides, I know exactly who they'd send when subtlety fails.

"I still have eighteen hours before you bring Phil in," Thane says, his voice carefully controlled but edged with something sharp.

The name hits the air like a blade.

Bree stops moving completely, and I watch her face cycle through recognition, terror, and then something worse—betrayal. She turns to look at Thane, and I can see the exact moment it hits her: he knew. He's known this whole time and didn't tell her.

"Oh, wonderful," Nyx purrs, noticing Bree's reaction. "I'm sure you're excited to be reunited, dear. He's been asking about you."

Thane's entire body is taut, silver eyes flashing with something close to panic before he locks it down.

"How thoughtful," I say, speaking for the first time since Nyx's arrival. My voice carries just enough lazy amusement to suggest I'm not taking any of this seriously. "The Council sending gifts."

Nyx's gaze flickers to me—brief, but loaded with meaning. She knows I'm hiding something, she has for a while. More importantly, she understands what I represent. The network I've built, even the possibility of what I could unleash.

She's counting on me not to interfere.

"Gifts," she repeats, tasting the word like wine. "Yes, I suppose you could call him that."

She takes a step back, preparing to leave as dramatically as she arrived. But her attention stays fixed on Bree, studying her with the kind of clinical interest that makes predators of us all.

"Enjoy your celebration," she says. "All of you. Such bonds are so rarely public. So rarely... permanent."

And then she's gone—shifting mid-leap, black wings carrying her back into the sky before anyone can respond.

The silence she leaves behind is deafening.

I watch Thane's face, catch the moment his carefully constructed control threatens to crack. He knows what's coming. Knows that Phil isn't just an "old friend"—he's the Council's hunter, their hybrid enforcer who's been circling Bree's life for years.

The others don't understand yet. But they will.

I push off from the doorframe, straightening as the crowd of Feeders slowly begins to lift their heads. They're looking to Bree for answers, for reassurance, for some sign that the Council's arrival doesn't mean the end of whatever hope they've found here.

But my thoughts aren't on them.

If Phil's coming, the board just got bloodier.

Good.

It's about time.

Chapter 11
BREE

I turn to stare at Thane, and the words echo in my head like a death knell.

Phil.

He knew Phil was coming.

Knew what happened.

Knew I was being hunted.

I didn't.

And he said nothing.

"You knew," I whisper, voice barely audible over the murmurs of the crowd still kneeling around us. "You knew he was coming."

Thane's silver eyes flash with something that might be regret, but it's too late. The damage is done.

"Bree—" someone calls from behind me. Rhett, maybe, or Gray.

"Wait, let us explain—"

"We can fix this—"

Something fractures inside me. Clean and sharp, like glass breaking along a fault line that was always there. The sound of their voices—concerned, urgent, trying to manage the situation they created—it's too much.

"No."

The Ether explodes out of me.

Power that swallows everything—the sanctuary doors, the crowd of Feeders, even the guys standing behind us. All of it disappears in a flood of silver light.

I stare into Thane's eyes, and for a moment I see both versions of him overlaid like double exposure—the man I let into my heart, and the man who kept me in the dark. The one who made me feel chosen, and the one who chose to betray me.

"How could you?"

The words are barely a whisper, but the Ether swells around us, responding to the fracture in my chest.

And just as quickly as it came, it all disappears.

When the mist clears, there's nothing.

Just endless black space dotted with distant stars, and a ground that feels like nothing but somehow holds me anyway. Empty except for me and him.

The silver strand still glows faintly between us, the only proof that any of this is real.

"Bree—" Thane starts, but I cut him off.

"Don't." My voice shakes with fury. "Just don't."

He takes a step toward me, hands raised like he's approaching a wounded animal. Maybe that's what I am. Maybe that's all I've ever been to any of them.

"I was trying to protect you—"

"Protect me?" The laugh that tears out of me has no humor in it. "By lying? By keeping me in the dark while you knew exactly what was coming for me?"

"You don't understand—"

"Then explain it!" The words rip out of my throat, raw and desperate. "Explain how you could stand there, bond with me, make me believe I could trust you—and the whole time you knew."

Thane's composure cracks, just slightly. "The others told me. They told Stellan and me everything about what happened with Phil, about what he did to you. I thought—"

The words hit me like a sledgehammer.

The others told me.

My knees nearly buckle as the full scope of the betrayal crashes over me.

"The others," I repeat, voice hollow. "Gray. Rhett. Jace. Wes. Theo." Each name tastes like ash on my tongue. "They all knew."

Thane's face goes carefully blank, which is all the confirmation I need.

"They knew... all of it. And none of them thought to tell me either."

"They were trying to protect—"

"Stop." The word comes out sharp enough to cut. "Just stop saying that."

The Ether writhes around me, responding to the storm building in my chest. I can barely think past the betrayal burning through my veins.

"I let you in," I whisper, wrapping my arms around myself. "All of you. For the first time in my life, I let people past the walls. I let myself believe I wasn't alone anymore."

"You're not—"

"Don't you dare!" The shout tears out of me. "Don't you dare tell me I'm not alone when you all decided I couldn't be trusted with the truth about my own life!"

Thane flinches, and something shifts in his expression—not just regret now, but alarm. His silver eyes track the mist coiling around us, and I see fear creep across his face.

"It wasn't about trust—"

"Then what was it about?" I take a step toward him, and the space around us trembles. "Because from where I'm standing, it looks like you all decided I was too weak, too broken, too fragile to handle knowing that one of my abusers was coming back for me."

Thane goes very still. "One of?" His voice is carefully controlled, but I catch the confusion underneath. "Bree, the mist—"

But I'm too lost in the wound they carved in my chest to pay attention to whatever he's seeing.

"You treated me like a child," I continue, the realization hitting with devastating clarity. "Like someone who needed to be managed instead of trusted. Protected instead of prepared."

Thane takes a step back, his gaze fixed on something I can't see, can't focus on past the betrayal consuming me.

"Maybe they were right to be afraid of me," I say quietly.

The space around us shudders at my words, and Thane's face goes pale.

"Maybe I was never meant to be trusted either."

"Bree, no—" His voice breaks, desperate in a way I've never heard from him. He reaches toward me, but stops short, like he's afraid of what his touch might do. "That's not—you can't believe that."

And from somewhere in the endless black around us, distant but unmistakable, comes the sound of laughter.

Soft. Maniacal. Pleased.

As if he'd been waiting for me to say it.

Chapter 12
WES

She's gone.

Fuck.

The space where Bree was standing is just—empty. Like she was never there at all. Like the Ether swallowed her whole and left the rest of us staring at nothing.

My chest caves in. Actually caves in, like someone reached through my ribs and scooped out everything that mattered. The absence hits me before my brain can even process what happened.

One second she was there, fury radiating off her in silver waves, demanding answers from Thane about Phil—*Phil, who I should have told her about, who I should have warned her was coming*—and the next, the world exploded in Ether light so bright it burned my retinas.

When it cleared, she was gone.

Just gone.

And the silence left behind feels like death.

"Bree?" Jace calls out, voice cracking on her name. He spins in a circle, hands outstretched like he could catch her if he just reaches far enough. "Bree, where—"

"She's not here." Theo's voice is hollow, distant. "I can't—I can't feel her."

Can't feel her.

My knees almost give out.

Because I can't either. The constant hum of awareness I've carried since the crown awakened everything—the way my magic always knew exactly where she was, like a compass needle pointing north—it's just... quiet.

Static.

Nothing.

"No." The word rips out of me, raw and desperate. "No, she's here. She has to be here."

I stumble forward, hands grasping at empty air where she was standing. Where the silver strand connected her to Thane just moments ago. But there's nothing. Not even a whisper of mist to prove she existed at all.

The crowd of Feeders who were kneeling around us is in chaos—some backing away from the spot where their Source just vanished, others pressing closer like proximity might bring her back. Their voices blend into a hum of confusion and panic that makes my skin crawl.

"Everyone inside." Stellan's voice cuts through the noise, sharp and commanding in a way that leaves no room for argument. "Now."

He doesn't wait to see if they listen. Just strides toward us, his usually perfect composure cracked enough that I can see the calculation running behind his eyes. Damage control. Crisis management.

But all I can focus on is the empty space where she should be.

"Wes." Gray's hand lands on my shoulder, solid and warm. "Come on."

I shake him off. "I'm not leaving her."

"She's not here," he says, gentler now. "Whatever happened, whatever the Ether did—she's not here anymore."

The words sink in, heavy and final. Because I know he's right. I can feel the wrongness of this space now, the way it tastes like absence instead of her.

But I can't make my feet move. Can't accept that she's just... gone.

"When did that happen?" I whisper, the question clawing its way up my throat. "When did she become—"

I stop. Because I can't say it. Can't put words to the realization that's been building in my chest for weeks now, getting stronger every time she looked at me like I'm more than what I've become.

When did she become everything?

When did losing her start feeling like losing myself?

"Inside." Stellan's hand closes around my arm, not rough but implacable. "Unless you want three hundred panicked Feeders to witness you fall apart."

He's right. I know he's right. But moving away from this spot feels like abandoning her all over again.

Stellan's grip tightens. "She's not here, Wes. But she's not gone forever." He pauses, something flickering across his expression—reluctance, maybe vulnerability. "I can still... sense her. Faint, but there. Whatever the Ether did, it didn't sever the connection."

The possibility that she's still out there, still connected, is the only thing that gets my feet moving.

The sanctuary feels too quiet as we file inside, like the building itself is holding its breath. Stellan guides us to a smaller chamber off the main hall—something that feels private, sacred, away from the chaos outside.

The door closes behind us with a soft click, and suddenly the weight of what just happened crashes down.

She's gone. Bree is gone, and it's because Thane kept secrets. Because we all kept secrets. Because I was so focused on hiding what I was becoming that I never told her about Phil, never prepared her for what might be coming.

My hands start shaking.

"I can't—" The words choke off in my throat. "I can't do this without her."

The admission hangs in the air like a confession. Because it's true. She's always been the center of everything—since we were kids, since before I understood what that meant. But these past few weeks, I finally stopped pretending otherwise. The thing that makes the hunger bearable, that makes the changes in me feel like growth instead of corruption.

Without her, I'm just—

Empty.

"Hey." Theo appears in front of me, calm and steady in that way of his that usually grounds me. "She's not dead, Wes. She's somewhere else."

"How do you know?"

"Because—" He gets that faraway look he gets when he's seeing something the rest of us can't. "I can still feel the echo of her. Faint, but real. She's not gone—she's just... somewhere else."

I stare at the thread, so faint I can barely make it out. But he's right. It's there.

"She's alive," Theo says quietly. "Wherever the Ether took her, she's alive."

The relief that floods through me is so intense it actually hurts. My knees do give out this time, and I sink into one of the chairs like all my strings have been cut.

Gray moves to the window, shoulders tense as he stares out at the crowd still milling around in confusion. "We need to figure out what happened. What triggered the Ether surge."

"Betrayal," Thane says quietly. It's the first word he's spoken since we came inside, and his voice sounds like broken glass. "She felt betrayed."

Jace whirls on him. "No shit. You think maybe that's because you *betrayed* her?"

"I was trying to protect—"

"Protect?" Jace's voice cracks with fury. "You knew Phil was coming for her and you said nothing. You let her walk into that crowd blind while her stalker circled like a fucking vulture."

"Enough." Stellan's voice cuts through the argument like a blade. "Fighting won't bring her back."

He moves closer, pacing near the window with focused intensity that makes my skin crawl. Like her disappearance is just another puzzle to solve.

"My guess?" he says, voice careful and measured. "The Ether responded to extreme emotional trauma. It didn't just hide her—I think it pulled her somewhere else entirely."

"Where?" Gray's question comes out rough, desperate.

"I don't know." Stellan's honesty somehow makes it worse. "But wherever it is, she's not unconscious. The bond is too active for that. She's... processing."

Processing. Like her disappearance into whatever space the Ether carved out is some kind of therapeutic retreat instead of a cosmic-level emotional breakdown.

"We have to bring her back," I say. The words come out steadier than I feel, but they're true. The panic is still clawing at my chest, but something else is building underneath. Something sharper.

"How?" Rhett asks from his spot by the door, where he's been standing guard like he expects Phil to burst through any second.

I look around the room—at Gray, whose eyes have that wild edge that makes my instincts go quiet, at Jace pacing like a caged animal, at Theo sitting too still, that careful blankness he gets when he's forcing himself not to feel. At Rhett by the door, hands flexed like he's ready for a fight.

They all feel it too. The wrongness of her absence. The way everything in this room feels half-formed without her presence to anchor it.

"I don't know," I admit. "But we figure it out. Together."

The words taste like a promise, and something in my chest settles into place. Like a decision made. Like a vow sworn.

Stellan nods slowly, something that might be approval flickering in his expression. "Good. Because wherever she went, she's going to need all of us to find her way back."

He pauses, glancing at each of us in turn.

"And something tells me we're going to need her more than she knows."

I can feel it then, faint but unmistakable—like an echo of her presence somewhere far away. For the first time since she disappeared, I let myself believe it might be possible.

She's out there. Somewhere in whatever space the Ether carved out for her to process the weight of our failures.

And we're going to bring her home.

She's ours. We're getting her back.

Chapter 13
THANE

I fucked up.

Bad.

The words hit hard, partly because I'm thinking them and partly because I just said them out loud. No silver tongue, no calculated deflection, no strategic positioning. Just raw, unfiltered truth.

"I fucked up. Bad."

Bree's still shaking beside me, silver mist snapping and crackling around her like live wire. But it's not just silver anymore—dark threads weave through it in patterns that make my skin crawl, black veins spreading through her Ether like infection. She doesn't seem to notice, lost in her fury and betrayal, but I can see it. The corruption threading through her power, turning something pure into something... else.

She's not looking at me—can't look at me, probably—and I don't blame her.

"Okay," I say to the endless black around us, voice pitched higher than usual. "Okay, so. This is new. This is definitely not covered in any Council handbook I've ever read." I run a hand through my hair, feel it shaking slightly. "Which is concerning because those handbooks are very thorough. Disturbingly thorough, actually. They have chapters on interdimensional travel, but nothing about—" I gesture vaguely at the star-dotted space. "Whatever this is."

A laugh escapes me, sharp and brittle. "Though I suppose 'how to survive after accidentally betraying a Source' wasn't exactly a priority topic when they were writing the manual."

That's when I hear it.

Soft. Amused. Predatory.

Laughter.

Not mine. Not Bree's.

Something else.

The sound cuts through the endless black around us like a blade, and suddenly I realize I've been so focused on Bree's explosion, on the silver strand still pulsing between us, on the weight of my own guilt, that I didn't actually look around.

I've been in crisis mode, tunnel vision locked on damage control. But now—

Now I lift my head and actually see where we are.

Nothing.

Endless black space dotted with distant stars that could be lights or could be eyes or could be nothing at all. The ground beneath our feet feels solid but looks like everything else here, like we're standing on a stage made of darkness itself.

And we're not alone.

The realization runs through me like ice water. That laugh—it came from somewhere. Someone. Something that's been watching us this whole time while I've been having my breakdown.

I clear my throat, trying to find some scrap of my usual control. "Uh… Bree?"

She doesn't respond. Still lost in whatever storm is raging inside her head, mist still crackling with those wrong-colored threads.

"Bree, where exactly did you take us?"

The voice that answers isn't hers.

"Nowhere and everywhere."

The words float through the darkness like smoke, each syllable deliberate and savored. The cadence is wrong—too slow, too careful, like whoever is speaking wants to taste each word before letting it go.

"Here, now… and then."

A chill runs down my spine that has nothing to do with temperature. I've heard predators before. I've been one. But this—this is something else entirely. Something that makes the word 'predator' feel inadequate.

Bree's head snaps up, confusion and fury blazing in her green eyes.

"The fuck?" she snarls, mist flaring brighter around her.

"No."

The voice cuts through her anger like silk over steel, gentle but implacable.

"Not yet."

The way it says those words—like a caress, like a promise, like a threat wrapped in velvet—makes every instinct I have start screaming at once.

Silence stretches between us and the darkness, heavy with presence I can't see but can feel watching. Evaluating. Waiting.

I thought I'd seen monsters. Thought I'd been one.

But this? This is something else entirely.

Wherever we are isn't empty.

It's occupied.

And whatever lives here has been waiting for us to arrive.

82

Chapter 14
THEO

Three hours past midnight and nobody's sleeping.

In the corner, Wes and Gray talk in hushed tones. Gray's hand rests steady on Wes's shoulder, voice low and calm as he tries to talk Wes down from whatever edge he's walking. The hunger is eating at Wes—I can feel it from here, sharp and desperate—but Gray doesn't flinch from it.

Rhett has completely dismantled some kind of mechanical device on the table, gears and springs scattered across the surface. His hands move with focused precision as he tries to put it back together, heat shimmering faintly around his fingers. It's the third thing he's taken apart tonight.

Jace sits cross-legged on the floor, muttering something about pancakes and how syrup should never be rationed in times of crisis. His usual manic energy has settled into something quieter, but his eyes stay sharp, tracking every movement.

Stellan paces near the window, phone pressed to his ear. His voice is too low to catch most of it, but fragments drift over: "...the nightmare... yes, now... how many..."

He catches me listening and turns away, but not before I hear him say, "Open the stable."

Thane isn't here. Hopefully he's with Bree, wherever they are. Both of them gone, leaving the rest of us to figure out how to bring them back.

I've been quiet but not because I don't know what to do.

Because I do.

I'm just afraid I won't come back from it the same.

But Bree? She's more important. She's everything.

I take a breath, steadying myself.

"I can find her."

The words cut through the restless energy like a blade. Everyone goes still—Wes stops mid-conversation, Gray turns from the corner, Rhett's hands freeze over his scattered gears, Jace looks up from the floor. I hear Stellan abruptly end his call.

Five sets of eyes fix on me, desperate and hopeful and afraid all at once.

"Theo," Gray says carefully, "what do you mean?"

I close my eyes, reaching out with my Seer abilities. If they're connected to this realm at all, if there's any thread of their presence left, I should be able to find it.

"She's not gone," I say, searching for any trace of connection. "They're not gone. They're just... displaced."

The moment I open myself fully to the vision, the world tilts.

Cold. Endless black. Stars that might be eyes. And Bree—

She's there, silver mist crackling around her, but it's wrong. Black threads weave through the light like infection, and something else moves in the darkness. Something that watches and waits and *hungers*.

Thane is beside her, but he's shaken, his usual composure cracked and bleeding panic.

I can feel it pressing at the edges of Bree's consciousness, whispering things I can't quite hear but know are poison.

"Bree."

My voice cuts through the Void, clear and strong. Not pleading—pulling.

She doesn't hear me at first. Too lost in whatever storm is raging inside her head, too overwhelmed by the presence circling them like a predator.

But I'm not letting her go.

"Bree." Louder this time, with all the conviction I possess. "You don't belong there."

In the sanctuary, I feel the others moving closer. Wes steps away from Gray, his hand landing on my shoulder, steady and warm. Gray moves up beside me, his presence solid and sure. Rhett abandons his scattered gears, and Jace stops muttering about pancakes. Even Stellan draws near.

We're all holding the connection now, each in our own way. All of us reaching for them.

"Come back to us."

It's not a request. It's a command, spoken with the authority of someone who sees truth and won't be denied.

In the darkness, Bree's head snaps up. Her eyes find mine across impossible distance, and for a moment the darkness around her recoils.

The thing in the shadows hisses—a sound like silk tearing—but I don't flinch.

"Come back," I repeat, gentler now but no less certain. "We're here. We're waiting."

The connection flares, silver light building between us, and for a moment I think I have them. I can feel Bree reaching back, Thane's desperation cutting through his panic—

But then something else cuts in. That voice, smooth and pleased.

"Oh, I don't think so."

The light fractures. The connection wavers, stretched thin but not broken.

In the blackness, I see Bree's eyes widen with fresh terror as the darkness presses closer. Thane moves to shield her, but whatever's there is stronger than both of them.

"Not yet, little queen." The voice is almost tender now, intimate in a way that makes my skin crawl. "We're not finished yet."

And then, directed at me—at all of us—a promise that feels like ice down my spine:

"I'll be seeing you real soon."

The vision cuts out like a severed cord.

I gasp, clutching my head as it pounds, vision blurring from the effort of reaching so far only to be slammed back.

"Theo!" Wes takes my arm. "What happened? Are they—?"

"They're alive," I manage, though my voice comes out rough. "But something's holding them there. Something that doesn't want to let them go."

The silence that follows is heavy with dread.

Whatever has Bree and Thane, it knows we're trying to reach them.

It might have won this time, but I'll keep trying. I have to.

Chapter 15
BREE

The echo of Theo's voice still vibrates in my bones—warm, steady, aching-ly familiar. For one perfect moment, I felt them all reaching for me across impossible distance. Wes's desperate hunger, Gray's fierce protectiveness, Rhett's burning certainty. Even Stellan's controlled concern threading through the connection.

But it's fading now, slipping away like water through my fingers.

And as reality crashes back in, so does the memory of what they did. What Thane did. The lies, the secrets, the way they all decided I couldn't handle the truth about Phil. About anything, really.

The warmth of their connection turns bitter in my chest. How can I miss them when they're the reason I'm here in the first place?

The black around us feels colder for its absence, pressing in tighter until I can barely breathe. The stars overhead—if they ever were stars—seem to pulse with malevolent awareness.

"Theo," I whisper into the endless dark, though I don't know why.

There's nothing. Just the suffocating weight of this place settling over me like a shroud.

Thane is beside me, silver eyes darting frantically as he searches for threats he can't see. His usual composure has shattered completely, leaving behind something raw and afraid. When he reaches for me, his hand shakes.

"We have to get out of here," he mutters, more to himself than me. "We have to—"

That's when the laughter comes again.

Soft. Amused. Predatory.

The sound curls around us like smoke, and I flinch so hard I nearly fall. Thane stiffens, moving instinctively to shield me, fangs extending as his body prepares for a fight neither of us understand.

"Not yet, little queen."

The voice that speaks is like velvet—deliberate, savoring every syllable like fine wine. The darkness begins to shift around us, not revealing a form exactly, but *suggesting* one. Sometimes I catch glimpses of a man's silhouette, sometimes something faceless and terrible. Sometimes both at once, flickering between states like a broken reflection.

Thane snarls, low and dangerous. "Show yourself, coward."

A chuckle drifts through the air, rich with amusement.

"Little feeder." The dismissal in those words makes Thane's jaw clench. "You've played your part admirably. The betrayal, the guilt—all of it fed her beautifully. But you can't shield her from me."

"Hey." The word snaps out of me before I can stop it. "Don't talk to him like that."

I'm furious with Thane. I hate what he did to me. But nobody gets to talk down to him like he's nothing. Not while I'm here.

The voice chuckles again, and I can hear the pleased surprise in it. "How protective. Even when the fire inside you rages because of what he's done."

Something about the way he says it makes my skin crawl. Like he can see right through me, right into the mess of anger and hurt I'm carrying around.

Thane's whole body goes rigid. I watch his face shift from panic to something colder, more calculating. The Thane I know snapping back into place as he realizes we're not just lost—we're being hunted.

The presence turns its attention to me, and suddenly the voice is closer, intimate, like lips brushing against my ear. I swear I can feel his breath.

"Welcome to the Void, little queen. Isn't it beautiful? In the way it consumes?" The voice says, sending a shiver through me.

"They kept the truth from you, didn't they?" Gentle. Understanding. Poisonous. "Decided you couldn't be trusted with your own fate. But I will trust you, little queen. I will tell you everything."

My skin crawls, but I can't deny the sick pull of his words. The way they echo every doubt I've swallowed, every fear I've buried.

"That darkness you fear in yourself?" His voice is almost tender now. "It isn't corruption. It's honesty. It's power. The power to take what you want instead of waiting to be given scraps."

The black threads in the Ether pulse brighter with every word, responding to something in his voice like plants turning toward sunlight.

"Who the fuck are you?" I snarl, summoning every scrap of defiance I have left.

The Ether flares silver, trying to burn him back. For one beautiful moment, it works—his form wavers, retreats—but then the black spreads again, stronger than before. The corruption threads through my Ether like veins, and part of me—a part I don't want to acknowledge—finds it almost soothing.

Thane goes deadly quiet. I can practically see him connecting dots, realizing just how deep this goes.

"I asked you a question," I demand.

The voice chuckles, pleased that I asked. "Names have power, little queen. To give one freely…"

I wait, and the waiting makes it so much worse.

"You may call me Ethos."

The name tastes bitter on my tongue, but it sticks there anyway. Like he branded it into my mind just by hearing it.

"Say it," he whispers. "It's already yours."

"No." But even as I refuse, the name echoes in my head.

Ethos. Ethos. Ethos.

"They will always fear you," he continues, circling me with words instead of footsteps. "Every time your power grows, they step back a little more. Whisper a little quieter. Wonder when you'll finally snap."

My chest tightens because he's not lying. I've seen it—the careful way they watch me, the gentle voices they use like I'm something fragile that might break.

"You give and give until there's nothing left," Ethos murmurs. "But I would take only what you choose to offer. I would never lie about what I am."

The black threads surge stronger, and for just a second, it feels like relief. Like finally admitting something I've been too scared to say out loud.

Maybe I'm tired of being the one who gives. Maybe I want to be wanted for something other than what I can do for everyone else. Maybe I want to take.

Thane must see something in my face because he grabs my arm. "Bree, don't. Whatever he's offering, it's not real."

"No, not yet." Ethos sounds bored now, like he's done playing. "You're not ready to choose. But you will be."

The darkness fractures around us without warning. The ground shatters like glass, and suddenly we're falling—

—crashing back into the sanctuary with a bone-jarring thud. Stone floor. Warm light. Voices shouting my name.

But his voice follows us back, soft and satisfied: "Sleep tight, little queen."

I'm shaking—not just from the impact, but from something deeper. My skin feels too tight, too sensitive, like every nerve is hyperaware. The warmth in my chest hasn't faded, and I hate myself for noticing, for wanting more of whatever that was.

When Wes reaches for me, his touch burns in a way that has nothing to do with his awakening magic. Everything feels too much, too intense. I can smell Gray's concern, hear Rhett's heartbeat hammering, feel Theo's exhaustion from his rescue attempt. Jace's eagerness to help.

And Thane—he takes one step toward me, hand half-raised as if to steady me... then stops. Pulls back just enough to make it look like he's giving me space, like it's for my sake. But I see the flicker in his eyes before the mask drops back into place.

Fear.

Chapter 16
RHETT

She's back.

I can't stop staring at her, can't quite believe she's real. One moment she was gone—vanished into whatever hole the Ether carved out for her and Thane—and now she's here, curled on one of the sanctuary's low couches like nothing happened.

Except everything happened.

I remember the hollow ache that followed her disappearance, the way the sanctuary felt wrong without her presence anchoring it. The frantic energy that consumed all of us, the desperate planning and the failed attempt to reach her.

And now she's back, but she isn't the same. I don't know why.

Her Ether coils close to her skin, silver mist threaded with something dark. Beautiful, yes, but wrong. Disturbing in a way that makes my instincts go quiet and alert.

The others must feel it too. Wes hovers nearby like he wants to touch her but doesn't dare. Gray's jaw is locked tight, his sharp eyes tracking every movement. Theo looks exhausted, drained from whatever he did to try and pull them back. Jace keeps starting conversations and abandoning them halfway through. Even Stellan watches from his position against the far wall, more interested than he lets on.

And Thane—

Thane looks like he's seen a ghost. Or become one.

"Where did you go?" Wes asks quietly, his dark eyes soft with concern.

"The Void," Bree says, like it leaves a bad taste in her mouth.

Stellan goes completely still. Not just quiet—frozen, like every muscle in his body has locked. His face drains of color, and for just a moment, his perfect composure cracks entirely.

"Stellan?" Thane's voice carries sharp concern.

"You were in the Void." It's not a question. Stellan's voice is barely above a whisper, and there's something raw in it none of us have heard before. "How are you—" He stops, jaw working. "How are you both still here?"

The way he says it makes it clear this isn't just about a dangerous place. This is personal. Terrifying.

"You know it," Bree realizes.

Stellan doesn't answer immediately. When he does, his voice is carefully controlled again. "I know what it does to people."

An uncomfortable silence settles over the room. Whatever the Void is, whatever happened there, it's worse than any of us understood.

No one presses for more details. There's an unspoken agreement hanging in the air: they're not ready to talk about it, and Stellan clearly has his own reasons for knowing about it. We can all wait.

Eventually, Stellan suggests rest. One by one, the others drift away—reluctant, but recognizing that crowding her won't help. Wes lingers the longest, his dark eyes full of concern, but even he eventually retreats upstairs.

I stay.

I always stay.

It's what I do—hold the line, keep watch, make sure she's safe even when she doesn't know she needs protecting. Especially then.

Bree shifts on the couch, drawing her knees up toward her chest. She's wearing one of my hoodies again—the gray one she claimed weeks ago and never gave back. Either that or the Sanctuary stole it for her. It swallows her small frame, the sleeves covering her hands completely.

"You don't have to babysit me," she says quietly, not looking at me.

"Not babysitting." I settle into the chair closest to the couch, close enough to reach her if she needs me. "Just staying."

She glances up then, and I see the exhaustion in her light green eyes. The kind of tired that sleep won't fix. Whatever happened in that void left marks on her—not physical ones, but deeper.

"I'm okay," she whispers.

We both know it's a lie.

But I don't call her on it. Instead, I just nod and lean back in my chair, making it clear I'm not going anywhere.

The silence stretches between us, not uncomfortable but heavy. The kind of quiet that carries weight.

After a few minutes, she shifts again—uncurling from her defensive position and sliding closer to the edge of the couch. Closer to me.

"Rhett?"

"Yeah?"

"Can you—" She stops, biting her lip. "Never mind."

"What do you need?"

She stares at her hands for a long moment, silver mist curling around her fingers. When she looks up, there's something vulnerable in her expression that makes my chest tight.

"I just want to feel safe for a minute."

The words hit me like a punch. Because I know what she's asking, and I know what it costs her to ask it. Trust doesn't come easy to Bree—it never has. But she's offering it to me anyway.

"Come here," I say softly.

She doesn't hesitate. Just unfolds herself from the couch and crosses the small space between us. For a moment she hovers, uncertain, and I realize she's waiting for permission.

I shift in the chair, making room, and she settles against me—tentative at first, then with growing confidence. Her head finds my shoulder, her body curving into mine like she belongs there.

Because she does. Even if she doesn't realize it yet.

The moment she settles against me, heat builds under my skin.

Shit.

The fire magic that's been awakening in me for weeks responds to the spike of emotion—relief that she's here, terror from almost losing her, protective fury at whatever hurt her in that void. It all tangles together and feeds the flames until my skin feels like it's burning from the inside out.

I should pull away. Should put distance between us before I burn her.

But she's shaking—fine tremors I can feel through the hoodie—and I'll be damned if I let fear make me abandon her when she needs me.

I focus on breathing. Deep, steady breaths that bank the fire instead of feeding it. I've been practicing this for weeks, learning to control the heat when emotions spike. Usually it works.

Usually I'm not holding the person who matters most in the world.

The temperature climbs anyway. I can feel it radiating through my shirt, warm enough that she has to notice. Any second now she'll pull away, ask what's wrong, and I'll have to explain that I'm a walking fire hazard who can't be trusted to—

Her mist curls around us both.

Silver light wraps around my arms, her waist, the space between us. And somehow—impossibly—it cools the worst of the heat. Not suppressing it exactly, but balancing it. Like the Ether recognizes the danger and steps in to protect us both.

Bree doesn't pull away. If anything, she relaxes further into me, her breathing evening out for the first time since she returned.

I wrap my arms around her carefully, still monitoring the heat levels, still ready to retreat if the fire spikes again. But the Ether holds steady, that cool silver presence keeping the flames in check.

"Better?" I ask quietly.

She nods against my shoulder. "How did you know?"

"Know what?"

"That this was what I needed."

I press my chin to the top of her head, breathing in the vanilla scent of her hair. "Because it's what I need too."

It's more honesty than I usually offer, but she deserves it. After everything—the disappearance, the fear, the relief of having her back—she deserves truth.

We sit like that for a long time. Her breathing gradually slows and deepens, the tension leaving her body bit by bit. The Ether continues to swirl around us, and I notice the black threads weaving through it are less prominent now. Still there, but subdued.

Whatever happened wherever the Ether took them, whatever those dark streaks represent, they seem quieter when she feels safe.

When she starts to drift toward sleep, I don't move. Don't shift to a more comfortable position or suggest she'd be better off in her own bed. I just hold her, keeping watch like I always do.

Her hand curls in my shirt, holding on even in sleep, and something fierce and protective rises in my chest.

"I've got you," I whisper, quiet enough not to wake her. "Always."

The fire under my skin has settled to a warm glow, controlled and contained by her trust in me. By the Ether's gentle intervention. By the simple fact that she chose me to keep her safe.

I stare at the ceiling, listening to her breathe, and make a silent vow.

I don't care what the black threads mean. I don't care what happened in that void or what darkness followed her back. She's here, she's safe, and I'll burn the world down before I let her vanish again.

The heat pulses once—not with panic this time, but with certainty.

She's mine to protect. And nothing—not fear, not fire, not whatever shadows are chasing her—is going to change that.

Chapter 17
BREE

I wake in the middle of the night, still wrapped in warmth—Rhett's hoodie, his lingering scent, the phantom memory of his steady breathing beneath my cheek. The sanctuary is deep in shadow, that heavy quiet that settles over everything in the small hours when even the ancient stones seem to hold their breath.

Rhett is asleep in the chair beside me, his broad frame somehow folded into the space, head tilted back against the cushion. Even in sleep, one hand rests near his leg like he's ready to reach for me if I need him. My chest tightens at the sight—this man who stayed awake to watch over me, who chose to sleep uncomfortably rather than leave me alone.

Who kept Phil's existence in this a secret for days, maybe weeks.

The betrayal hits fresh, sharp as a blade between my ribs. Not just Rhett. All of them. Rhett, Gray, Jace, Theo, Wes, Thane, Stellan. Every single one of them knew Phil was coming for me and decided I couldn't be trusted with the truth. Decided I was too fragile, too breakable, too much of a liability to handle my own life.

Yesterday that knowledge felt like drowning. Like proof that no matter how much they claimed to care, I'd always be the one they managed instead of trusted.

But as I sit here, the Ether stirring restlessly around my feet, something else rises beneath the hurt. Something far more complicated.

My body aches in ways that have nothing to do with physical injury. The Void left marks on me—not visible ones, but something deeper. Like parts of me were touched that shouldn't be, awakened that should have stayed sleeping.

The black threads are still there, woven through my silver mist like veins. I can feel them even now, subtle and dark, threading through the Ether that pools around my ankles. They don't hurt. That's what disturbs me most.

They feel like honesty.

That darkness you fear in yourself? It isn't corruption. It's power.

Ethos's words echo in my mind, and I hate how they settle into place like they belong there. Like they were always true, just waiting for someone brave enough to say them out loud.

I need to move. The sanctuary responds to my restlessness before I'm even fully upright—corridors shifting subtly to guide me away from Rhett's protective sleep, stones humming with that gentle silver warmth. But tonight it feels insufficient. Like trying to fill an ocean with a teaspoon.

That's when I hear the pacing.

I follow the sound toward the kitchen, bare feet silent on the cool stone floors. The sanctuary guides me through hallways that seem shorter tonight, more direct, like it understands the urgency thrumming under my skin.

Wes stands in the kitchen, moving back and forth like a caged animal. His dark hair is disheveled, sleep shirt wrinkled, and there are shadows under his eyes that speak of hours spent awake. He looks wrecked—beautiful and desperate and barely holding himself together.

The moment he sees me, he stops.

"I thought you were gone for good."

The words burst out of him before I can say anything, raw and desperate. His voice cracks on the last word, and I hear everything he's not saying: the terror, the relief, the need so sharp it's almost physical.

Something in my chest responds to that honesty. To the way he's not trying to manage me or protect me from his own feelings. He's just laying himself bare, trusting me to handle it.

You give and give until there's nothing left.

But maybe I'm tired of being the one who only gives.

Instead of keeping my distance like I usually would, I step closer. One deliberate step, then another, until I'm close enough to see the gold flecks in his brown eyes, close enough to feel the heat radiating from his skin.

"I'm here," I say quietly. "I'm not going anywhere."

Wes searches my face like he's looking for proof, for some sign that I mean it. Whatever he finds there seems to undo him completely.

"Bree, I—" He stops, jaw working. "I can't do this without you. I don't know how to be without you."

The admission hangs between us, vulnerable and electric. I can feel his hunger radiating off him in waves—not just for food anymore, but for connection. For me. The awakening magic in him calls to something deep in my chest, something that wants to answer.

The words steal my breath. No one has ever said that to me before—not like this. Not with such raw honesty that it feels like he's handing me his heart and trusting me not to crush it. I've spent my whole life being too much for people, watching them step back when I needed them most. But

Wes is stepping closer, making himself vulnerable, choosing me even when it costs him.

Their lies still sting. The way they all decided what I could handle, what I deserved to know. But standing here with Wes, seeing the raw need in his eyes... their betrayal feels smaller somehow. Less important than this moment where someone is finally being completely honest with me.

The power to take what you want instead of waiting to be given scraps.

For once, I don't want to wait for him to decide I'm strong enough or ready enough or worth the risk. I don't want to wait for permission from anyone.

I reach up and cup his face in my hands.

"Then don't be without me."

His eyes widen almost in disbelief under my touch, like he can't believe I'm real. Like he's afraid one wrong move will make me disappear again.

"Bree," he whispers, my name a prayer and a question all at once.

I answer by kissing him.

It's desperate from the first moment—messy and hot and hungry in a way that has nothing to do with gentleness. Wes kisses me back like he's drowning and I'm air, his hands fisting in Rhett's hoodie, pulling me closer until there's no space left between us.

This isn't the careful comfort Rhett offered last night. This is raw need, the kind that burns through pretense and leaves only truth behind.

The moment our tongues meet, something shifts in the air around us. I feel the Ether responding to the contact—warmth rising from my skin, but different than usual. Instead of the gentle curl I'm used to, it rushes outward, pouring into him. I can feel threads of energy sinking beneath his skin, igniting something that was waiting just beneath the surface.

The pull at my Ether is gentle but unmistakable. Familiar.

I've felt this before.

With Thane.

I pull back, breathless, staring up at Wes as understanding crashes over me. "You're feeding from me."

His eyes widen, then close as if in defeat. "Yes."

"You're—" I pause, the word catching in my throat.

His jaw tightens like he's bracing for me to flinch. "Say it."

"You're a Feeder," I whisper. Not a question this time.

He nods, opening his eyes to meet mine. "Incubus-class, like Stellan. But different." His voice cracks on the admission, quiet but raw. "I wasn't going to tell you. I thought... if you knew, you'd look at me different. Like everyone else does."

His voice is quiet, uncertain. "I don't fully understand how it works yet, but I know the deeper the connection, the closer I am to someone—" He pauses, searching for words. "The more it sustains me. The hunger quiets."

Understanding floods through me. "That's why it gets worse when you're alone. Why it eases when you're with us."

"With you," he corrects. "It eases when I'm with you." His hands find my waist, gentle but certain. "Everyone else helps a little, but you—" He stops, struggling to explain something he doesn't fully understand himself. "You're different. Essential."

"And just now, when we kissed—"

"The moment I felt close to you, really close, the hunger just—it took over. I couldn't stop it." His eyes search mine. "I don't know exactly what I'm taking from you, but I know I need it. And I know this is only the second time I've actually fed."

"Second time?"

He blushes—actually blushes—and looks away. "I fed from Gray. Just a little. It was an accident, we were—" He stops, color deepening across his cheekbones. "We were close, and it just happened."

I pause, processing this. Gray and Wes. The image shouldn't affect me the way it does, but heat curls low in my stomach. Not jealousy—something else entirely. Something that makes my pulse quicken and my breath catch. Heat that belongs to Wes's confession, to the thought of Gray, to both of them together.

"Are you okay with that?" he asks quietly, misreading my silence. "I know it's weird, and I didn't mean for it to happen—"

"I'm not afraid of what you are, Wes. I don't want less because of it—I want more. Of you. Of this."

His eyes widen slightly. "Really?"

"Really." I step closer, drawn by the honesty in his confession, by the vulnerability of admitting he'd been intimate with Gray. "Tell me what it was like."

But instead of answering, he searches my face with something like wonder. "You're not pulling away. You know what I am, what I need, and you're not running."

"No," I say, reaching up to cup his face again. "I'm not running."

"Bree—"

"I felt it with Thane too. The pull, the exchange. But this is different." My thumb traces his cheekbone, and he leans into the touch like he's starving for it. "With him, it felt... controlled. Careful. This feels like need."

"It is need," he admits, voice raw. "I need you so much it scares me."

"When I get close, I can feel it building. If I don't control it, it can overwhelm... both of us."

His eyes flick to mine, dark and unsteady. "But with you—it doesn't feel like losing control. It feels like giving you exactly what you need."

The honesty in his words, the vulnerability, makes something fierce rise in my chest. Here he is, admitting to being something the magical world considers lowest, confessing to a hunger he can't control, and all I want to do is give him more.

The power to take what you want instead of waiting to be given scraps.

"Then take what you need," I say, and before he can protest, I kiss him again.

The hunger simmers between us, unresolved and electric. Promise of more to come. I can feel it in the way he's looking at me now—not like I'm something fragile that might break, but like I'm powerful enough to choose what I give and when.

Like I'm powerful enough to take what I want, too.

The moment stretches, charged and perfect, until footsteps echo down a distant corridor. Someone else is awake, moving through the sanctuary in the deep hours of night.

Wes and I exchange a look—loaded with everything we can't say, everything we're not ready to explain to the others yet. Not when they're still the ones who lied to me. Not when I'm finally learning what it feels like to take instead of waiting to be given.

But as I watch him run a hand through his disheveled hair, still looking slightly stunned by what just happened, one thought settles into my mind with crystalline clarity:

For once, I didn't wait for their permission. I took what I wanted. And it felt like power.

The black threads in my mist pulse once, as if in agreement.

And somewhere in the sanctuary's depths, I notice the absence of silver eyes and controlled composure. Thane hasn't come looking for me. Hasn't reached out since the Void. And maybe the part that scares me most is how little that scares me now.

Chapter 18
WES

I can't sleep.

Not after the kitchen. Not after the taste of her Ether flowing into me like liquid starlight, filling hollows I didn't know existed until they were suddenly, impossibly full.

The hunger that's been clawing at me for weeks is sharper now—not worse, but more focused. Like it finally knows what it wants. Like it finally knows what it's been waiting for.

Her.

I pace the length of my room, bare feet silent on the cool stone. The sanctuary responded to me when I moved in, shaping the space around my needs—soft textures, warm colors, a bed built for comfort rather than just sleep. But tonight it all feels too small, too contained for the restless energy thrumming under my skin.

Every time I close my eyes, I see her face in the kitchen. The way she looked at me when I admitted I'd fed from Gray. Not jealous or hurt—*aroused*. Like the thought of me with him turned her on instead of threatening her.

"Tell me what it was like," she'd said, and her voice had gone rough with want.

Christ. What is she doing to me?

I run my hands through my hair, trying to shake off the memory. But it clings, stubborn and intoxicating. The way she stepped closer instead of pulling away. The way she chose to kiss me again after learning what I was.

The way she let me feed.

A soft sound interrupts my spiraling thoughts—the quiet click of my door opening. I turn, expecting maybe Theo with another vision, or Rhett checking on everyone like he does when he can't sleep.

Instead, it's Bree.

She stands in the doorway barefoot, dark hair mussed, still wearing Rhett's oversized hoodie. But there's nothing uncertain about her posture. Nothing hesitant or questioning.

She looks at me like she's made a decision.

"I don't want to wait anymore," she says quietly.

The words hit me like lightning. Direct. Certain. So different from the careful, cautious Bree who usually second-guesses every choice.

"Bree." My voice comes out rougher than I mean it to. "You don't have to—"

"I know I don't have to." She steps into the room, closing the door behind her with deliberate care. "I want to."

The air between us shifts immediately, charged and thick. I can feel her Ether stirring, silver mist beginning to curl around her ankles, and my hunger responds with a sharp spike of need.

She crosses the room slowly, never breaking eye contact. When she's close enough to touch, she stops.

"In the kitchen, you said you needed me," she says. "Show me how much."

The last of my restraint snaps.

I reach for her, cupping her face in my hands, and kiss her like I'm drowning. She kisses me back just as desperately, her hands fisting in my shirt, pulling me closer until there's no space left between us.

The moment our mouths meet, the Ether responds. I feel it rushing from her skin into mine, warm and electric and intoxicating. But this time I don't panic. This time I let myself sink into it, let myself *take*.

The feeding is different now—not the accidental pull from before, but something deliberate. Controlled. I can feel her pleasure sparking through the connection, can sense every gasp and shiver like it's my own.

And I realize something that makes my breath catch: the more pleasure I give her, the more she gives me in return. It's not taking at all—it's creating something beautiful and desperate between us, where every gasp she gives me makes me want to give her more.

"Wes," she breathes against my mouth, and I can hear the surprise in her voice. Like she's feeling the same connection I am.

"I know." I trail my lips down her throat, tasting vanilla and starlight on her skin. "I can feel it too. Every time you let go a little more, I feel it. And you like it, don't you?"

She makes a soft sound that's half gasp, half moan, and the Ether surges brighter. I can taste her surrender in the magic flowing between us, sweet and electric on my tongue.

"Don't hide from me," I murmur against the sensitive spot where her neck meets her shoulder. "I can feel when you're holding back. And I want everything you'll give me."

Her hands slide under my shirt, nails dragging across my skin in a way that makes me shudder. "Then take it."

The words hit me like lightning—so different from the careful, hesitant Bree I'm used to. There's something new in her voice, something bold and unapologetic that makes my pulse spike. I can feel it in the Ether too, black threads weaving through the silver in patterns I don't understand. But right now I don't care about the source. Right now I only care about the way she's looking at me like she's finally ready to stop apologizing for what she wants.

I lift her easily, her legs wrapping around my waist as I carry her to the bed. The hoodie rides up, and I realize she's only wearing underwear beneath it—the thought makes my mouth go dry and my hunger spike so sharp it's almost painful.

When I lay her down, she doesn't look away or try to cover herself. She just watches me with those light green eyes gone dark with want.

"Tell me what you need," I say, my voice dropping to that low register that makes her breath catch.

"You." The word comes out without hesitation. "All of you. I'm tired of being careful."

Something fierce and possessive rises in my chest. "Then we won't be careful."

I pull her hoodie over her head, and she helps me, lifting her arms without a trace of self-consciousness. The sight of her bare skin in the dim light makes my mouth go dry, makes the hunger spike so sharp it's almost painful.

But I force myself to go slow. To worship every inch of exposed skin with my mouth and hands until she's arching beneath me, silver mist rising from her skin like steam.

I trail kisses down her throat, tasting vanilla and starlight on her skin. Her pulse flutters under my lips, and when I find that sensitive spot where her neck meets her shoulder, she makes a soft sound that sends fire straight through me.

"You're beautiful," I tell her, and I can feel the truth of it resonating through the magical connection between us. "So fucking beautiful."

I map the curves of her waist, her hips, the soft skin of her thighs. Every touch sends sparks through the Ether, doubling the sensation until I can barely think straight. My fingers trace the edge of her underwear, pulling a gasp from her lips

When I hook my fingers in the waistband of her underwear, she lifts her hips to help me slide them away. No hesitation. No fear. Just trust and want and the kind of raw honesty that makes my chest tight.

She reaches for my shirt then, and I let her strip it away, let her explore the planes of my chest and stomach with curious hands. Every touch sends sparks through the Ether, making us both gasp at the intensity.

"Wes." My name on her lips sounds like prayer and demand all at once.

"I'm here." I settle between her thighs, pressing kisses to her hipbones, her inner thighs, anywhere I can reach. "I'm not going anywhere."

The first touch of my mouth makes her cry out, her back arching off the bed as pleasure crashes through the Ether. I can feel her sensation like it's my own, can taste her pleasure on my tongue, and it's intoxicating.

I work her slowly, thoroughly, using the magic to read exactly what she needs. Every gasp and moan feeds back into my hunger until I'm drunk on the taste of her, on the way she comes apart in my mouth.

"Don't stop," she gasps, her hands tangling in my hair. "Please don't stop."

"Never," I promise against her skin. "I could do this forever."

And I could. The way she responds to me, the way her pleasure feeds directly into my hunger—it's perfect. Sustainable. Like we were made to fit together exactly like this.

When she comes the first time, the Ether explodes around us in a shower of silver light threaded with black. I feel her climax like an electric shock, feeding me so completely that for a moment I can't breathe.

But it's not enough. Not nearly enough.

I kiss my way back up her body, savoring every tremor and aftershock. When I reach her mouth, she kisses me desperately, tasting herself on my lips.

"More," she whispers against my mouth. "I want more."

"Greedy," I tease, but there's approval in my voice. Pride. "I like that. I want you greedy."

She reaches between us, her hand wrapping around me with a confidence that makes me groan. "Then give me something to be greedy about."

I nearly lose it right there. The combination of her touch and her words and the way the Ether is singing between us—it's almost too much.

But I want to savor this. Want to make it last.

I capture her wrists, pinning them gently above her head. "Patience. We have all night."

"I don't want to be patient." There's an edge to her voice now, something demanding that makes my pulse spike. "I've been patient my whole life. I'm done waiting."

The words hit me hard because I can hear the truth in them, can feel the shift in her through our connection. This isn't just about sex—it's about power. About choosing what she wants and taking it without apology.

"Then don't wait," I tell her, releasing her wrists to frame her face with my hands. "Take what you want from me. All of it."

She surges up to kiss me, and this time there's nothing soft or hesitant about it. She kisses me like she's claiming me, her nails dragging down my back hard enough to leave marks. She hooks her legs around my thighs, pulling me to her.

When I finally sink into her, we both cry out. The sensation is overwhelming—not just physical, but magical. I can feel her pleasure mixing with mine, creating something bigger than either of us alone.

I move slowly at first, savoring every sensation, every gasp and moan. But she won't let me stay gentle.

"Harder," she demands, her legs wrapping around me again to pull me deeper. "I won't break."

"No," I agree, my voice gone rough with need. "You won't."

I give her what she wants—what we both need. Deep, claiming strokes that make her arch beneath me, that send lightning through the magic until I can't tell where I end and she begins.

The black threads in her Ether pulse brighter with every thrust, weaving through the silver until her magic looks like dark starlight. It should worry me. Instead it just makes me hungrier, makes me want to drive her higher until she's completely undone.

"That's it," I breathe against her ear. "Let go. Let me feel all of it."

She comes apart in my arms with a cry that sounds like my name, her body clenching around me as the Ether explodes between us. The feeding is so intense it borders on overwhelming—wave after wave of her pleasure crashing into me until I'm dizzy with it.

But I'm not done with her yet. I slow my movements, drawing out her aftershocks, my mouth finding that sensitive spot on her throat that makes her gasp. I can feel her body responding again, the magic sparking back to life as I build her toward another peak. The Ether thrums between us, silver and black threads pulsing in rhythm with our bodies.

"Say my name," I command, my voice rough with need. "Say my name when you let go."

"Wes," she gasps, and then again, louder: "Wes!"

I feel her body tighten around me, her pleasure crashing through our magic like a wave of pure light.

My own climax follows seconds later, ripping through me with an intensity that leaves me shaking. For a moment the world goes white, everything reduced to pleasure and magic and the feeling of being completely, impossibly full for the first time in my life.

We collapse together afterward, breathing hard, her head pillowed on my chest. The Ether settles around us like a blanket, still sparking with aftershocks—silver threaded with those dark veins that pulse like a heartbeat.

I'm full. Truly, completely full for the first time in my life. The hollowness that's been eating at me for weeks is gone, replaced by a warm, thrumming energy that makes my skin feel electric. I'm half-stunned by the intensity of it, half-drunk on the sensation of being exactly what I was meant to be.

"Your pleasure feeds me, Bree," I whisper against her hair, the words spilling out before I can stop them. "That's what I am. And I'll never stop wanting more."

She makes a soft sound of contentment, her fingers curling in my shirt like she's anchoring herself to me. Her breathing is already slowing, eyelids heavy with satisfaction and exhaustion.

Watching her like this—sated, trusting, completely undone in my arms—something shifts in my chest. The possessive hunger sharpens into something fiercer. More protective.

She chose me. Fed me. Made me powerful instead of broken.

But it's more than that. Her trust is what makes this possible—without it, I'm nothing but hunger. Without her choosing to give, I'm just another predator taking what isn't mine.

The weight of that responsibility settles over me, heavier and more precious than any power.

I pull the blankets up around her carefully, tucking her against my side. She doesn't stir, just burrows closer with a sleepy sigh that makes my chest tight with something I don't have words for yet.

No one touches her, I think, the vow crystallizing with surprising intensity. *No one takes from her without her choosing it. She's mine to feed from, mine to protect.*

The thought should probably scare me—the raw possessiveness of it, the way it feels carved into my bones. Instead it just feels right. Natural. Like this is what I was always meant to become.

Bree's breathing evens out completely, one hand still fisted in my shirt like she's afraid I'll disappear if she lets go. But I don't move. Don't want to break the connection, don't want to disturb the perfect weight of her against me.

I should be tired. Should be ready to sleep off the overwhelming intensity of what just happened.

Instead I'm buzzing with restless energy, my new strength crackling under my skin like electricity looking for somewhere to go. The feeding satisfied the desperate hunger that's been clawing at me, but it's also awakened something else. Something that feels too big to contain in this room, no matter how perfect the moment is.

I stare at the door, a slow grin tugging at my mouth.

The night isn't over yet.

Chapter 19
Gray

The sanctuary usually swallows sound.

Tonight it handed me hers.

I've been staring at the ceiling for hours, replaying every sound that shouldn't have made it through these walls. Her voice, soft and desperate. The way she called his name—*Wes*—like it was torn out of her.

This place keeps secrets. Thick stone, older than anything I understand. Most nights, I can't even hear footsteps in the hallway. But tonight felt different. Like the house wanted me to lie here with my jaw clenched and my hands fisted in the sheets, knowing exactly what was happening down the hall.

My teeth ache. Every muscle feels coiled too tight, like I'm ready to spring or fight or run. Something's been crawling under my skin for weeks, and tonight it's clawing to get out.

I should feel guilty about the way my pulse jumped every time she made those sounds. Should be ashamed of how much I wanted to be the one pulling them from her lips.

But guilt isn't what's eating at me.

It's hunger. Raw and getting worse every time I replay her voice in my head. And underneath that—something I won't look at too closely—is the way I keep thinking about *him*.

Wes.

About the sound of his voice responding to her, too quiet for words but satisfied. About what he probably looks like right now, loose and glowing and carrying her scent.

About how much I want to see that up close.

The knock is soft. Hesitant.

My heart kicks against my ribs like it's trying to break free. This is it—the moment I've been circling around for hours, maybe weeks. The chance to stop wanting and start taking.

I know who it is.

When I open the door, Wes slips inside like he was waiting for permission. The sight of him stops me cold—hair messed up like his fingers kept running through it, his mouth swollen, even his shirt is buttoned wrong. Not because he was rushing. Because he dressed while still half-gone from whatever happened with her.

And he still is. Half-gone. There's something dreamy in his expression, like part of him is still back in her room, still feeling her hands on his skin. His eyes have that soft, unfocused look that comes after really good sex, when your body remembers every touch even as you're trying to function normally.

But there's something else. Something that makes me look twice.

His face looks different. Sharper. The line of his jaw, his cheekbones—everything that was already good-looking about him has been turned up. It's subtle, but I've known him long enough to notice.

Then the scent hits me. My nose catalogs it before I can stop it: sex, satisfaction, Bree's vanilla sweetness all over his skin. Arousal and sweat and something floral that's probably her soap. It's obvious and intimate and makes something possessive snarl in my chest.

"Couldn't sleep," he says with that crooked grin, but he's practically glowing with satisfaction. There's something different in the way he holds himself—looser, more confident.

The room feels smaller with him in it. Charged, like the air before a storm.

"Good night?" I ask, because the evidence is written all over him and I need to hear it.

His cheeks flush deeper, and that grin turns almost shy. "Yeah. Really good."

I close the door behind him, turn the lock. The sound seems too loud in the quiet room.

"She wear you out?" He blinks, that dreamy look sharpening as he realizes what I just asked.

"I—how did you…?" A pause, uncertainty flickering across his face. "Gray, did you—?"

"Lucky guess," I say, watching him process. But then that grin returns, wider now, almost giddy.

"God, Gray. It was… I can't even…" He runs a hand through his hair, making it worse. "I mean, it's Bree. And she wanted—" He stops, shakes his head like he still can't believe it happened. "Just can't settle after… that, her, you know?"

I do know. But this feels different from his usual restless energy. More charged, like he came here specifically, not just because he was wandering.

He moves toward the window, then changes direction toward the bed, then stops in the middle of the room like he can't decide where he belongs.

That restless energy is back, but it feels different now—less desperate, more like he's waiting for something. For me to make a move.

The jealousy I've been choking on crystallizes into something sharper, more focused. Something that demands action.

I close the distance between us in two steps, crowding him back against the wall. My hands brace against the surface on either side of his head. He goes still but doesn't try to move. If anything, he leans into it.

"I heard her," I say, voice rougher than I meant. "Every sound."

His breath catches. "Gray—"

"I want to know what Bree tastes like."

The words are out before I can stop them. Raw and desperate and loaded with months of buried want. It's my excuse, my permission slip to finally touch him - but it's not a lie. I do want her. I want them both. This is just the only way I can let myself reach for one through the other.

Heat flickers in his expression. He knows what I'm asking.

"Take her from me," he breathes.

I don't hesitate. Kiss him hard, desperate. Because I am. He responds immediately, melting against me with a sound that makes something fierce flare in my chest. His hands fist in my shirt, pulling me closer.

He tastes like salt and heat and Wes. But underneath, I can taste her. Vanilla lip balm, and something sweet. Proof he was with her first.

It should bother me. Instead, it makes me hungrier. I deepen the kiss like I'm claiming him and the echo of her.

"More," I growl, and he nods.

"Whatever you want."

I search his face for hesitation. There's none. Just want and trust and something that looks like relief.

"Strip."

He doesn't hesitate, pulling his shirt off in one motion. The sight of him—chest flushed, faint scratches that weren't there this morning—makes my mouth go dry.

But as I'm looking at him, something shifts. The excuse I used to get here starts feeling thin. Because yes, I can taste her on his lips, smell her sweetness on his skin. But what's making my heart race isn't the echo of her.

It's *him*. The way he's breathing hard. The way he's looking at me like he's been waiting for this. The way he's standing there trusting me completely.

Something wakes up in my chest. Something that's been sleeping under careful control for months. The excuse crumbles, leaving nothing but raw want and an instinct I don't recognize but can't ignore.

Mine.

Not *I want him. He's mine.* Mine to claim, mine to take apart. The possessiveness hits like a punch, so intense I can barely breathe.

"Bed." Not a request.

He moves without question. I follow, watching every line of his body like I'm memorizing it. When he settles on the mattress, looking up at me with dark eyes and swollen lips, something inside me snaps.

I settle over him without touching. Close enough to feel his heat, count his breathing. The careful control I've kept around him dissolves.

"You're mine now," I tell him. Not a question.

His pupils blow wide. His breathing stutters. "Gray..."

"Say it."

"I'm yours." Breathless, eager. "And hers."

The surrender unlocks something primitive. Something that recognizes submission and responds with certainty. I kiss him again, deeper, claiming his mouth like I own it.

Maybe I do.

I work my way down his body slowly, deliberately, mapping every response and cataloging every place that makes him gasp or arch beneath me. His skin is warm and salt-sweet under my tongue, and I take my time learning the taste of him - the hollow of his throat where his pulse races, the sensitive spot just below his collarbone that makes him shiver.

When I finally take him in my mouth, he makes a sound that goes straight through me—raw and grateful and completely undone. His hands thread through my hair, not pulling or pushing, just holding on like I'm the only thing keeping him grounded.

I lose myself in the weight of him on my tongue, the way his breathing goes ragged when I do something he likes. And then I taste it—really taste it. Not just the faint vanilla from his lips, but something deeper, more intimate. The sweet-salt taste of her, still there from where she touched him, where her mouth was on him. It's unmistakable and it hits me like a punch to the gut.

I want her too. The thought crashes over me with startling clarity. This isn't just about claiming Wes or tasting an echo of her. I want Bree—want to know what she tastes like directly, want to feel her come apart under my tongue the way Wes is doing now. The realization should probably terrify me, but it doesn't. It just makes everything sharper, hungrier.

I work him with renewed intensity, chasing both tastes—his and hers—like I can somehow have them both through this. Every response feeds something desperate in my chest, something that's been starving for both of them without me even realizing it.

"Gray," he gasps, voice breaking on my name, hands tightening in my hair. "I'm not gonna last."

"Don't want you to," I tell him, pulling back just enough to meet his eyes. "Let go for me."

When he comes, it's with my name torn from his throat and his hands still fisted in my hair. I work him through it carefully, savoring every tremor, every broken sound, until he's boneless and panting beneath me.

I wonder if she can hear it. If the sanctuary is handing her my voice the way it gave me hers.

I'm nowhere near done.

The thing that's awakened—this need to claim and possess—is hungrier now.

"My turn," I say when he reaches for my clothes.

His eyes sharpen when he sees my expression. "What do you want?"

"Everything." I reach for the drawer, grab what I need. "All of you."

Heat flickers in his face. "Yes."

"You sure? This changes things."

"Good. I want it to change."

I settle between his thighs, wanting to see his face this. I prepare him carefully, starting with one finger, watching his face for every reaction, every flutter of his eyelashes. He's responsive from the first touch, breath catching as I work him open slowly, methodically.

"More," he asks after a few moments, voice already going rough around the edges.

I add a second finger, scissoring gently, and his back arches off the bed. The trust in his eyes is almost overwhelming - the way he's completely open to me, letting me set the pace even when I can see he wants more, wants it faster.

"You sure you're ready?" I ask when he starts rocking down against my hand.

"Gray, please," he breathes, and I can feel how he's trembling with want.

I add a third finger, taking my time to stretch him properly, and he makes a sound that goes straight through me. His thigh trembles under my free hand as I work him open, watching the way his pupils dilate, the way his breathing goes shallow and quick.

"That's it," I murmur, feeling the way his body yields to me. "Just let me take care of you."

When I finally press into him, we both go very still. He takes me inch by inch, breathing carefully through the stretch, his hands gripping my shoulders like he's anchoring himself to me. The connection is intense, intimate in a way that goes beyond just physical. Finally I'm fully seated and we're both holding our breath like we're afraid to break the moment.

"Okay?" I ask, voice strained with the effort of holding still when every instinct wants me to move.

"More than okay," he breathes, eyes dark and trusting. Then he rocks his hips up to meet me and whatever control I had left evaporates completely.

I set a rhythm that's careful but insistent, deep enough that he feels every stroke, slow enough that we both feel every point of connection. He meets me thrust for thrust, his body opening for me like this is what he was made for, like we've been building toward this moment for years. The sounds he makes are different now—deeper, more vulnerable, like I'm touching places in him that no one else has ever reached.

This isn't about Bree anymore. Hasn't been since the moment I backed him against the wall. This is about the way he looks at me like I'm the only thing in the world that matters. About the way he gives me his complete surrender without question or hesitation. About the way something deep in me recognizes something deep in him and claims it without apology.

"Show me," I murmur against his neck, not even sure what I'm asking for.

But he knows. He gives me everything—his body arching beneath mine, his submission takes my breath away. When he comes again, it's with my name torn from his throat and his nails digging into my shoulders.

I follow him over a few thrusts later, burying my face in his neck as everything goes white-hot and perfect, like coming home to something I didn't know I'd been missing.

After, I make myself move even though every instinct wants to stay buried in him. I wipe us both down with careful hands, press a glass of water into his palm because it's the only way I can touch him gently right now without starting this all over again. My protective instincts are sharper now, more focused, like they've been honed to a fine edge. When I try to give him space to process what just happened, he pulls me back down beside him.

"Don't go anywhere," he says, voice soft but certain.

I settle against him, let him arrange us how he wants. The possessive thing in my chest has gone quiet, satisfied for now. It's patient, certain this is just the beginning.

"Definitely need a new headboard," he says after a while, flexing his fingers where he gripped the wood.

I laugh, surprised by how easy it feels. "We'll make Rhett do it. Add it to his list."

"Think he'll ask questions?"

"Probably. Won't get any answers, though."

He hums in agreement, already half-asleep against my chest. I hold him as his breathing evens out, as the sanctuary settles around us with what feels like contentment. As if it approves of what it started.

I should be thinking about what this means, how it changes everything.

Instead, all I can think about is how right this feels. How the thing under my skin has finally gone quiet.

I thought tonight was about Bree—about chasing the echo of her through him. But what I found was Wes. And in claiming him, I uncovered a part of myself I didn't know I'd been waiting for—the part that doesn't ask, doesn't hesitate, doesn't apologize. He's mine now. Not because I took him, but because he gave himself to me. And that should probably terrify me. Instead, it settles into my bones like it's always been there, like it was inevitable.

I hold him tighter, already knowing this won't be the last time.

Chapter 20
JACE

Pancakes.

Golden, fluffy, not-burned-to-a-crisp pancakes.

I flip the last one with theatrical flair, landing it perfectly in the center of the pan. "Behold," I announce to the empty kitchen, spatula raised like a sword. "Pancakes. Golden. Edible. No fire alarms. You're welcome."

The victory tastes sweeter because of recent disasters—like yesterday morning when I got distracted and burned a whole batch because I walked in on Gray and Wes having what was definitely not a casual conversation in the pantry. Let's just say my focus has been... divided lately.

But today? Today I kept my eyes on the pan and my mind on the task.

And this? This is redemption served hot with syrup. And butter. Lots and lots of butter.

I stack the pancakes on a platter, admiring my handiwork. Perfect golden circles, evenly cooked, fluffy as clouds. Cooking is one of the few things that actually calms me down—there's something therapeutic about the rhythm of mixing batter and flipping flapjacks when you know what you're doing. Keeps my hands busy and my brain focused on something other than the chaos swirling around this place.

What the hell is happening in this place lately?

The sanctuary's been... different. Charged, like the air before a storm. Everyone's walking around like they're carrying live wires under their skin. Something shifted after the whole Phil revelation, after Bree's trip to the Void with Thane. The energy feels thicker, more electric.

Don't overthink it. Just make pancakes.

I focus on plating instead. Stack the pancakes just so, arrange the bacon in neat rows, pour fresh orange juice into glasses. Simple tasks that keep my mind from wandering down paths that probably lead to more questions than answers.

Footsteps on the stairs—Rhett and Theo, judging by the rhythm. Early risers, both of them. Probably been up for an hour already, doing whatever responsible people do at dawn.

"Morning," Rhett says as he appears in the doorway, hair slightly mussed but otherwise looking like he got actual sleep. Lucky bastard.

Theo follows, looking more rumpled than usual. His shirt's buttoned wrong and there are pillow creases on his cheek. "Something smells incredible."

"Feast your eyes," I say, gesturing dramatically at the spread. "The breakfast of champions. Or fugitives. We'll see how the day goes."

Rhett's mouth quirks in what might be a smile. "Impressive."

"I have my moments." I pour coffee into two mugs, sliding them across the counter. "Don't look so surprised. I can handle basic kitchen duties without causing property damage."

"Most of the time," Theo adds, settling onto one of the stools.

"Hey, that lasagna was an *experiment*."

"A disaster," Rhett corrects, but there's warmth in his voice.

"I was testing the smoke alarm's reliability."

More footsteps on the stairs—Thane's measured pace, unmistakable even from a distance. He appears in the doorway looking like he slept about as well as I did, which is to say not at all. His usually perfect composure is slightly rumpled around the edges.

"Coffee," he says without preamble, like it's a prayer.

"Coming right up," I say, pouring him a mug. "You look like hell."

"Charming as always, Langston." But there's no real bite to it. He accepts the coffee like it's a lifeline.

More footsteps—multiple sets this time. I know without looking that it's the trio who've been practically orbiting each other for weeks. The tension's been building so thick you could cut it with a knife.

Bree appears first, moving slower than usual. She's wearing what looks like Gray's shirt—definitely his, it's way too big and smells like cedar even from here—and her hair's doing that thing where it looks artfully messy instead of just messy.

Then Wes, whose face has that soft, slightly dazed expression that comes after really good—

Nope. Not going there.

Gray brings up the rear, and I have to do a double-take. There's something different about him. Something in the way he moves, like he's finally settled into his own skin after years of fighting it. His eyes catch the light when he glances around the kitchen, just for a second, and I swear they flash with something that definitely isn't human.

When the hell did everyone get a magical upgrade while I was flipping pancakes?

"Please tell me that's coffee," Bree says, voice rough with exhaustion.

"Coffee, pancakes, bacon, and orange juice," I announce. "The full spread. Because apparently, y'all look like you need feeding."

She pauses halfway to the counter, and I catch the way she glances at Wes and Gray. Not guilty, exactly. More like she's checking to make sure they're okay. Like whatever happened between them was intense enough to require aftercare.

Holy shit.

"Busy night?" I ask, eyebrow raised, because I apparently have no filter when I'm operating on three hours of sleep.

Bree nearly chokes on her first sip of coffee. Wes flushes bright red. Gray just glares at me like he's considering throwing something sharp in my direction.

And then Stellan—because of course he chooses this exact moment to grace us with his presence—walks in carrying his own mug and catches the tail end of my question.

He takes one look at the three of them, glances at Thane's rigid posture, then at me, and bursts out laughing.

Not his usual controlled chuckle or that razor-sharp amusement he uses like a weapon. This is genuine, unrestrained laughter that echoes off the kitchen walls and makes everyone jump.

"Oh, I like this one," he says, wiping at his eyes. "Subtle as a brick to the face."

Thane shoots Stellan a look that could freeze fire, but there's something almost relieved in his expression. Like he's grateful someone else is acknowledging what he's seeing.

"I aim to please," I mutter, but I'm grinning now too. Because Stellan laughing—really laughing—is like watching a marble statue crack jokes. Rare and weirdly endearing.

Bree buries her face in her coffee mug. "Can we please just eat?"

"Absolutely," I say, because watching her try to disappear into her breakfast is almost as entertaining as watching Gray contemplate murder. "Dig in, people. Food's getting cold."

Rhett and Theo exchange one of those looks—the kind that says they're having an entire conversation without words. Whatever they're thinking, it's serious enough to make the easy morning atmosphere shift.

"We can't just sit here," Rhett says finally, his voice carrying that no-nonsense tone that means he's thinking tactically. "We need a plan. Do we run, or do we face Phil?"

The name drops into the conversation like a stone in still water, sending ripples of tension through the room. Bree goes very still, her knuckles white where she grips her mug.

"Can we just eat?" she asks again, but there's an edge to her voice now. A warning.

"We can't ignore this forever," Theo says gently. "The Council knows where we are. Phil's coming. We have maybe hours before—"

"Before what?" Bree cuts him off. "Before we have to choose between running like criminals or fighting a war we're not ready for?"

The debate heats up from there. Theo advocating for strategic retreat—the sanctuary won't shield them forever, they need mobility, options. Rhett pushing for defensive positioning—protect Bree, regroup, make them come to us. Gray suggesting they go on the offensive—confront Phil before he can make the first move, his eyes flashing again as he speaks.

I try to lighten the mood. "So option one: road trip. Option two: death match. Option three: I make more pancakes and we pretend none of this is happening?"

Nobody laughs this time.

That's when I really look at them. *Really* look.

Bree's got this faint glow about her, like she's lit from within. It's subtle, but once I notice it, I can't unsee it. Silver light just beneath her skin, pulsing faintly with her heartbeat.

Wes looks... sharper. Like someone took an eraser to the softer edges of his features and left behind something that catches the eye. His cheekbones could cut glass, and when did his jaw get that defined? "Since when are your cheekbones sharper than mine?" I mutter, staring at him.

But it's Gray who really makes me pause. When he talks about confronting Phil, his eyes don't just catch the light—they glow. Faint, but definitely there. Like something wild and predatory is looking out through his face.

I nearly drop my fork. "When the hell did everyone get a magical upgrade while I was flipping pancakes?"

The table goes quiet. Too quiet.

"You noticed," Stellan says, voice carrying that familiar note of amusement mixed with something darker.

"Hard not to," I say, gesturing vaguely at the three of them. "Bree's practically glowing, Wes looks like he stepped out of a magazine, and Gray's eyes are doing that thing where they're definitely not human anymore."

Bree touches her face self-consciously. "Glowing?"

"Like someone put a dimmer switch under your skin and turned it up," I confirm. "It's subtle, but it's there."

The silence stretches, heavy with implications I'm not sure I want to understand.

"The bonding," Theo says quietly, like he's putting pieces together. "It's changing all of you."

"Into what?" Gray asks, and there's an edge to his voice that makes my instincts sit up and pay attention.

"Into what you were always meant to be," Stellan answers. "The Ether doesn't just awaken magic—it evolves it. Deepens it. Makes it stronger."

Thane's gone completely still, his silver eyes fixed on Bree with an intensity that makes the air feel charged. There's something in his expression—not anger, exactly, but a kind of predatory focus that makes my skin prickle.

Stellan looks directly at me. "The question is: what happens to those who haven't bonded yet?"

The words hit like a slap. Because he's right, isn't he? The Ether has chosen most of us—I can see it in the way Gray's eyes flash, in Rhett's steady heat, in the restless energy crackling around the room. Hell, it chose me too, along with all the others. But bonding? That's different. That's Bree's choice. And so far, she's only made that choice once.

With Thane.

Which leaves the rest of us in some kind of limbo.

"They look like they didn't sleep," I say instead of addressing the elephant in the room. "In the good way, if you know what I mean." I wiggle my eyebrows for emphasis.

Because it's true. Underneath the glow and the sharpened features and whatever magical evolution is happening, they all look exhausted. Worn down. Like whatever they shared last night took more out of them than they're admitting.

Bree's eyes dart between Wes and Gray, and I watch something like panic flicker across her face. She looks at Wes first—soft, almost protective—then at Gray, and her expression shifts to something more frantic.

"I wasn't—" she starts, then stops, color draining from her cheeks. "Gray and I didn't—we weren't together. Not like—"

The words hang in the air, and I realize what she's just done. She's confirmed she WAS with Wes while trying to clarify she wasn't with Gray.

Thane's coffee mug hits the counter with enough force to crack the ceramic. His silver eyes have gone cold as winter, fixed on the black threads in her mist with something that looks dangerously close to recognition.

"After the Void," he says, voice deadly quiet. "You were with him after the Void."

It's not a question.

Bree sets down her coffee mug with deliberate care, but her hands are shaking. "We can't run forever."

The subject change is desperate, obvious, but the words settle over the table like a blanket anyway, smothering the tension that was building. Everyone looks at her—not as someone fragile who needs protection, but as someone stepping into authority. Into power.

Into whatever the hell she's becoming.

About time.

She continues, voice steadier now despite the panic still flickering in her eyes. "We can't. And I'm tired of being afraid. Tired of hiding. Tired of letting other people make choices about my life."

Gray's eyes flare brighter at her words. Wes leans forward like he's drawn by invisible threads, but there's worry in his expression now—like he's starting to understand why Thane looks ready to commit murder. Even Rhett's protective tension shifts into something more focused, more purposeful.

She's not just talking about Phil. She's talking about everything—the Council, the sanctuary, the bonds that are changing all of them in ways they don't fully understand.

"So what do you want to do?" I ask, because someone has to break the tension before Thane explodes.

She looks around the table, meeting each of our eyes in turn. When her gaze lands on me, I see something that makes my chest tight—determination mixed with trust, like she's counting on me to be exactly who I've always been even as everyone else becomes something new.

"We face them," she says. "Together. Whatever comes next, we face it together."

The table goes quiet again, but it's a different kind of silence. Charged with possibility instead of fear.

Maybe the real question isn't whether we run or fight. Maybe it's whether we can keep up with her at all.

Because looking at Bree now—glowing, determined, stepping into power that was always hers, those black threads pulsing through her silver Ether—I'm starting to think she's not the one who needs protecting anymore.

We are.

Chapter 21
BREE

"You don't have to be unafraid," Theo says quietly, his hand steady on my shoulder. "You just have to stand."

We're still inside the sanctuary, clustered near the main doors, and I can hear the murmur of voices outside. The whole community gathering. Waiting.

For me.

My hands won't stop shaking.

"I can't," I whisper, staring at the heavy wooden doors like they're the gates of hell. "Theo, I can't face him. Not after—"

"Yes, you can." His voice is calm, certain. "You've already survived him once. You're stronger now."

"Am I?" The question comes out broken. "Because I feel like that same terrified girl who used to hide when he came knocking."

Theo moves to stand in front of me, his dark eyes serious. "That girl survived. That girl found the strength to leave, to build something new. She brought all of us together." His voice drops. "She's still in there, Bree. And she's not weak."

I close my eyes, trying to breathe. Trying to believe him.

"The community is scared," I manage. "They need me to be strong, and I—"

"They need you to be real," Theo corrects. "Fear doesn't make you weak. It makes you human."

The doors creak open, and Gray appears. His face is grim. "He's here."

My stomach drops. Everything inside me goes cold and small.

Phil.

"Bree?" Theo's voice sounds far away, even though he's right in front of me.

I can't move. Can't speak. The air feels too thin, like I'm drowning on dry land.

You don't have to be unafraid. You just have to stand.

The words echo in my head, but they feel meaningless against the panic crawling up my throat.

Someone takes my arm—Rhett, maybe, or Gray—and guides me toward the doors. My legs move without conscious thought, carrying me forward even though every instinct screams to run.

The sunlight hits my face like a slap.

And there he is.

Phil stands just outside the sanctuary gates, hands clasped behind his back. That same predatory smile. That same easy confidence. The man who pretended to be just my landlord while installing cameras in my bathroom. While watching me, hunting me, waiting.

The sight of him hits me harder than I expect. My vision narrows until there's nothing but his face, his voice, the memory of his hands on me that time at my apartment. The smell of alcohol and cigarettes, the way he pressed too close, spoke too softly about "arrangements" we could make about rent.

I can't breathe.

Can't think.

Can't—

"Breathe, darling." Stellan's voice cuts through the fog, sharp and unyielding. "He doesn't deserve your silence."

His words aren't gentle or comforting but they're just enough of a shock to drag me back to the present.

I suck in air, the taste of it sharp and real. My hands are still shaking, but I can feel my fingers again. Can feel the ground under my feet.

Phil's smile widens as he watches me struggle to compose myself.

But something's wrong. This isn't the Phil I remember—the drunken, slovenly landlord who reeked of alcohol and stale cigarettes. This man is lean, handsome even, wearing a tailored suit jacket and expensive-looking pants. His posture is straight, confident, predatory. No trace of the stumbling drunk who used to leer at me in hallways.

Nothing is the same except his eyes. Those cold, calculating eyes that used to watch me through my apartment window.

The transformation makes my stomach turn. How long was he pretending? How much of what I thought I knew was a lie?

"There she is," he says, voice carrying easily across the space between us. "My favorite tenant. Looking good, as always."

The possessive tone makes my skin crawl. Around me, I'm dimly aware of the community gathering—families with children, elderly couples, all the Feeders who came seeking sanctuary. But they feel distant, like I'm watching them through glass.

"Phil." The name comes out steadier than I expect.

"You look well," he continues, like we're having a pleasant conversation. "This place agrees with you. Though I have to say, I'm disappointed. When I heard you'd become some kind of queen, I expected... more."

His gesture takes in the crowd behind me. I don't turn to look, but I can feel their fear like a weight against my back.

"These are the followers you've gathered? Broken Feeders and frightened families?" Phil's laugh is soft, almost fond. "Oh, sweetheart. Trying to save them? You couldn't even save yourself."

The words cut deep, not because they're untrue, but because there's enough truth in them to hurt. These people are scared. They are broken. And maybe I am too.

The Ether around my feet flickers, silver light dimming. The black threads that have been woven through it since the Void pulse like a heartbeat, dark veins spreading through the silver mist.

Phil's eyes lock onto the corruption threading through my power, and his smile turns genuine for the first time. Hungry.

"Beautiful," he breathes, like he's looking at something precious. "Daddy will be so pleased to see how well you're coming along."

A low growl rumbles from somewhere behind me, sending a shiver down my spine. Thane.

Phil's eyes flick past me, and his smile turns cold. "Watch it, boy. Remember your place."

Then his attention returns to me, dismissive and final. "Come quietly," Phil says, extending one hand. "This little spectacle has gone on long enough. It's time to stop playing pretend."

The reasonable tone makes my skin crawl. Because I know what lies underneath it. I remember what reasonable got me in my apartment. What it cost me every day I lived under his roof.

My heart hammers against my ribs so hard I'm sure everyone can hear it. The light at the edges of my vision makes the world feel wrong, tilted, like I'm standing on the deck of a sinking ship.

You don't have to be unafraid. You just have to stand.

Theo's words echo in my head, and I cling to them like a lifeline.

"No." The word comes out barely above a whisper.

Phil's smile doesn't waver. "I'm sorry, what was that?"

"No." Louder this time. The Ether swirls higher around my feet. "I'm not going anywhere with you."

Something flickers in Phil's expression. Not anger—amusement.

"Now, Bree. We both know how this ends. You can make it easy on everyone, or..." His gaze shifts to the crowd behind me. "Well. Let's just say these people have already suffered enough, don't you think?"

The threat is clear. Comply, or watch him hurt the people I've tried to protect.

My vision starts to blur at the edges. The familiar panic rising, threatening to pull me under.

Stand. Just stand.

"Leave them alone," I manage. "This is between us."

"Is it?" Phil takes a step forward, onto sanctuary ground. "Because from where I'm standing, it looks like you've dragged all these innocent people into your mess. Made them targets."

Each word is a knife between my ribs. Because he's not wrong. They are here because of me. In danger because of me.

"That's enough," someone says behind me—Rhett, his voice tight with anger.

But Phil doesn't even glance at him. His focus stays locked on me, like a predator watching his prey.

Zira appears at my side, her presence steady and fierce. "You heard her," she says, voice cutting through the tension. "She said no."

Phil's smile widens as he takes in this new player. "And who might you be?"

"Someone who's tired of men like you," Zira replies coolly.

"Adorable," Phil says, dismissing her with a glance. "But this is business."

"You were always so dramatic," he continues conversationally, speaking to me again. "Making everything harder than it needed to be. Remember what I used to tell you about keeping quiet? About being a good tenant?"

I do remember. The cameras. The threats. The way he'd lean too close and breathe alcohol into my face while explaining what would happen if I caused trouble.

The panic claws higher, making it hard to think, hard to focus. The world starts to feel unreal, like I'm watching it happen to someone else.

Phil's magic hits without warning.

Green light. Pain splitting through my skull. I'm on my knees, gasping.

"There we go," Phil says. "Much better."

I try to get up, but the magic makes it impossible to think straight.

"Now then," Phil says, taking another step closer. "Let's try this again."

He reaches for me, fingers inches from my arm.

"Take her."

The command comes from behind Phil, directed at someone I can't see through the haze of pain and fear.

Footsteps approach. Gentle hands close around my arms, lifting me to my feet.

Seth.

Relief crashes through me. He's helping. He's—

Phil starts laughing.

The sound cuts through everything—my relief, my gratitude, my desperate hope that someone is finally standing up to him.

Seth's grip shifts, becoming less supportive and more restraining. His body is still between me and Phil, but suddenly that feels like a cage instead of protection.

"Get your hands off of her," Thane snarls from somewhere behind me—furious and too late.

Phil's laughter grows louder, delighted.

"Oh, this is perfect," he says, wiping at his eyes. "Did you see her face? That moment of hope before she realized?" His smile turns almost fond. "Daddy always said you were too trusting."

Seth doesn't look at me. Doesn't look at anyone. Just holds me in place while Phil savors the moment.

"You really thought he was one of yours," Phil continues, his voice warm with mock sympathy. "Poor Bree. Still so naive, even after everything."

The mist around my feet goes wild, silver and black flickering between rage and panic. But it doesn't matter. Nothing matters.

Because Seth—quiet, helpful Seth who walks with me through the grounds and asks about my day—is holding me for Phil like I'm cargo to be delivered.

Silence. No one moves. No one speaks.

And Phil's laughter rings out over it all, delighted and terrible and final.

"We don't run," I'd said this morning, standing in that kitchen sur-rounded by people I thought I understood. But here I am, being held by someone I trusted while everyone else stands frozen.

The words taste like ash now—hollow and meaningless as everything else I thought I knew.

The sanctuary didn't fall today.

It was never really safe to begin with.

Chapter 22
THEO

Seth's hands on Bree's arms.

Phil's laughter echoing off the sanctuary walls.

The Ether around Bree's feet convulsing—silver light shot through with black threads that pulse like a wound.

I watch it all unfold with the horrible clarity that comes when time slows down and you can see exactly how everything is going to break apart.

Make the right choice, I will Seth silently. *Let her go. Step away.*

But Seth doesn't step away. His grip on Bree shifts, and I catch the smallest curve of his lips. Not regret. Not even cruelty.

Satisfaction.

My stomach drops. This isn't coercion. This isn't him being controlled or threatened.

He wants to be here.

Fuck.

Thane moves first.

A snarl rips from his throat as he lunges forward, fangs flashing, silver eyes blazing with fury. For a moment he looks exactly like what he is—a predator unleashed, dangerous and deadly.

Phil raises one lazy hand.

Thane hits an invisible barrier and flies backward, slamming into the ground ten feet away. The impact drives the air from his lungs in a harsh gasp. He tries to get up, muscles straining, but the magic holding him down is absolute.

"Stay," Phil says conversationally, like he's talking to a disobedient dog.

The humiliation on Thane's face is devastating. This is someone who's spent centuries as an apex predator, reduced to struggling helplessly in the dirt.

Stellan doesn't lunge. He calculates.

"You always did enjoy easy prey," he says, voice cutting through the tension easily. "Tell me, does it make you feel powerful? Terrorizing children and broken Feeders?"

Phil doesn't even glance at him. Just continues holding Bree's gaze while Seth keeps her trapped.

The dismissal hits Stellan and I watch his perfect composure crack, just for a moment. Something cold and sharp flickers in his expression.

Fear.

Real fear.

Because if Phil can ignore Stellan—who commands respect through pure presence alone—then none of us matter to him at all.

Zira steps forward, raising her voice above the crowd's horrified murmurs.

"He's one man!" she shouts, fierce and desperate. "He doesn't own us!"

For a heartbeat, it almost works. Murmurs ripple through the gathered Feeders. A few shift forward, remembering their courage.

Phil's eyes land on Zira, and his smile turns lazy. Amused.

"Little leech," he says, voice dripping with disdain. "Still trying to play revolutionary?"

The crowd recoils. The brief spark of defiance dies as quickly as it came.

Mairen and Torn step forward, flanking Bree protectively. Their son Kellan moves with them, young face set with determination.

"Don't," someone hisses from the crowd. "Don't make it worse."

Hands grab at them, pulling them back. Neighbors who sought sanctuary together now choosing safety over solidarity.

"Please," Mairen whispers as she's dragged away from Bree's side. "She's just a girl."

But the fear is too strong. One by one, the people who came here seeking protection choose to protect themselves instead.

I know what's coming now. I wish I didn't.

Gray's transformation starts violent and desperate. Bone cracks and reshapes beneath his skin. Fur erupts along his arms in patches of white. His eyes go completely inhuman, wild and feral.

Phil watches with mild interest, then flicks his wrist.

Gray crumples mid-shift, gasping as the magic forces his body back to human form. The incomplete transformation leaves him writhing on the ground, caught between shapes and in agony.

"Uncontrolled," Phil observes. "Pathetic, really."

Rhett's fury ignites the air around him. Heat waves ripple outward, scorching the grass at his feet. The temperature spikes so fast that people near him stumble backward, sweat beading on their foreheads.

Phil just laughs.

"Wild magic," he says dismissively. "No finesse. No discipline."

The flames gutter out like someone blew out a candle.

Jace's knives lift from their sheaths, spinning in tight circles as air currents catch them. His power builds, ready to send them flying—

They clatter to the ground.

"Did you really think parlor tricks would work on me?" Phil's voice carries genuine amusement. "I've been hunting your kind for decades, boy."

Wes moves last.

His hunger surges outward, but not to feed. Instead, it carries emotion—raw, desperate feeling that crashes over the entire crowd like a wave. Fear and grief and longing so pure it takes my breath away.

For a moment, everyone feels it. The weight of what we're losing. The desperation of watching someone you care about slip away.

People gasp. Some stagger. Even Phil pauses, his confident expression flickering.

"Daddy doesn't care about feelings, parasite," he says after a beat, but there's less certainty in his voice now.

Wes collapses to his knees, drained by the effort.

I watch it all with growing horror. Each attempt, each failure, building a wall of helplessness that threatens to bury us all.

But my mind is already moving past the immediate crisis, cataloging what Phil doesn't know:

He crossed onto sanctuary ground minutes ago. Stepped right over the boundary like it was meaningless.

The Ether around Bree isn't just convulsing—it's reaching. Stretching toward something beneath our feet.

The sanctuary itself is stirring. Not just the building, but the land. The stones in the walls hum with energy I've never felt before. The trees in the garden lean inward like they're listening.

Phil thinks he's won because he overpowered us individually.

But he doesn't understand what he's really facing.

Seth's grip tightens on Bree's arms, and she looks up at him with such devastation that something breaks in my chest. The betrayal is written across her face in stark, brutal lines.

But underneath the hurt, I see something else.

The same thing I felt when she touched the crown in the attic bedroom. When the voice called her queen and power flooded through her like recognition.

She's not just standing on sanctuary ground.

She's standing on land that belongs to her.

And it's starting to remember.

The air tastes metallic, like a storm breaking. The soil itself hums under my boots with barely contained power.

Our eyes meet across the space between us. Hers are bright with unshed tears and dark with fury. But there's something deeper there too. Something that makes the air around us thrum with possibility.

He stepped onto your domain, I repeat, and somehow I think she hears it. *Now show him what that means.*

Chapter 23
BREE

Where are they?

The thought circles through my mind like a mantra as Phil's laughter echoes off the sanctuary walls. Gray, Rhett, Jace, Wes, Theo—I can't see any of them in the crowd. Can't feel their presence the way I usually do, that warm anchor that tells me I'm not alone. And Thane, Stellan—where are they?

What if Phil hurt them? What if they're lying somewhere bleeding while I'm trapped here, helpless? The possibility makes my chest seize with panic that has nothing to do with my own safety and everything to do with theirs.

I need them. I need to know they're okay, need to see their faces, need—

Seth's hands on my arms feel like shackles.

Phil's laughter echoes off the sanctuary walls, bouncing back at us from every direction until it fills the air like smoke. The crowd presses against the buildings, a sea of faces watching our destruction unfold.

I can't breathe past the panic clawing up my throat. Can't think beyond the way Seth's fingers dig into my skin—not cruel, but firm. Certain. Like he has every right to hold me here while Phil circles us like a predator.

"Let go of me," I whisper.

Seth's grip tightens. Not painful, but deliberate. His hands are warm and steady, the same hands that helped families at the border. The same hands that gestured gently as we walked through the garden, making me feel like I had a friend who understood.

The same hands that are now keeping me trapped.

"Let go of me." Louder this time.

Phil's smile widens. "Oh, I don't think he will, Bree. You see, he's been very patient. Very loyal." His eyes flick to Seth with something like approval. "Haven't you, Seth?"

Patient. Loyal.

The words crawl into my skin and stay there. How long has Seth been patient? How long has he been loyal—to Phil, not to me?

Every quiet conversation we've had over the past weeks flashes through my mind. Every time he asked how I was doing, every gentle question about my day, every moment I thought someone actually cared about me without wanting something in return.

Was any of it real?

"How long?" The question tears out of my throat before I can stop it. "How long have you been lying to me?"

Seth doesn't answer. His face remains calm, gentle even. But there's something different in his eyes now. Something that was always there, maybe, but I was too grateful for kindness to notice.

Distance. Calculation. The look of someone playing a role.

"Such a dramatic little thing," Phil says, and his voice carries that same reasonable tone he used to use when he'd corner me in my apartment hallway. When he'd explain why the rent was late and what I could do to make up for it. "Always making everything so much harder than it needs to be."

The Ether stirs around my feet, responding to the fear and rage building in my chest. Silver light flickers, shot through with black threads that pulse with power.

"You have no idea what you are, do you?" Phil continues, stepping closer. "What you could become with the right guidance. Daddy's been so looking forward to meeting you properly."

Daddy. The word sends ice through my veins. Not Phil, then. Someone else. Someone worse.

The ground beneath us trembles.

"All those times you helped around the sanctuary," I say to Seth, my voice cracking. "All those conversations in the garden, all those times I showed you around because I thought you cared. Was it all just... surveillance?"

Something flickers across Seth's face. Not guilt, exactly. Maybe regret. But not the kind that comes from hurting someone you care about. The kind that comes from a job becoming more complicated than expected.

"Did you report everything?" I press, desperation bleeding into my voice. "Every conversation, every moment I trusted you, every time I let my guard down? Did you tell Phil about all of it?"

The silence stretches between us, heavy and damning. Seth's grip on my arms shifts slightly, and I catch the smallest curve of his lips. Not cruel, but satisfied. Like he's exactly where he wants to be.

Like this moment—my terror, my betrayal, my complete helplessness—is what he's been working toward all along.

The realization breaks something inside me.

Not the gentle kind of breaking that heals clean. The violent kind that leaves jagged edges and makes you dangerous.

"You were supposed to be safe," I whisper.

The Ether responds to my words, silver light climbing higher around us. But the black threads are spreading through it like poison, and the air begins to taste of metal and lightning.

"You were supposed to be different."

The crowd shifts restlessly. People step back, sensing something building. Even Phil's confident expression flickers as the temperature around us drops.

"You were supposed to be *mine*."

The last word comes out raw, desperate. Because that's what hurts the most—not that Seth was working for Phil, but that I thought I finally had someone who was just mine. Someone who chose me without wanting to use me or break me or reshape me into something else.

Someone who saw me as worth protecting instead of worth hunting.

But there is no one like that. There never was.

My eyes find them in the crowd—Gray's face twisted with something that might be fear, Rhett's hands clenched uselessly at his sides, Jace looking younger and more lost than I've ever seen him. Wes pale and shaking. Theo's usual calm shattered. Even Thane and Stellan, hanging back with expressions I can't read.

Even them.

The realization fractures whatever I had left.

The ground splits beneath my feet, hairline cracks spreading outward like a spider web. The ancient stones in the sanctuary walls begin to hum, power flowing through them like they're remembering something they'd forgotten.

"Let go of me," I say one more time.

Seth's hands tighten. "I can't do that, Bree."

His voice is gentle. Apologetic, even. But his grip doesn't loosen.

And that's when I understand that he's not going to let me go. That Phil isn't going to stop. That no one is coming to save me because the person I thought might try is the one holding me prisoner.

I scream.

The Ether explodes outward like a star going nova.

Silver and black light erupts in every direction, tearing through the air with a sound like the world splitting open. The sanctuary responds instantly—stones crack in the walls with reports like gunshots, ancient timber groans and splinters, the very foundations of the building shudder.

The power doesn't just destroy. It transforms.

Where the silver light touches, impossible flowers bloom from cracked stone. Where the black threads reach, the ground turns to obsidian glass that reflects nothing. The two forces war with each other, creation and destruction locked in perfect, terrible balance.

The earth bucks beneath us like a living thing. Cracks spread outward from where I fall to my knees, radiating through the courtyard in a pattern that looks almost like wings. The air itself burns, crackling with energy that makes every nerve in my body sing.

Glass shatters in every window of the sanctuary. The crowd cries out, hands pressed to their ears as the sound of raw magic tears through the space like breaking metal. Some collapse to their knees. Others run.

And through it all, the sanctuary's ancient power awakens.

The building doesn't just respond to my Ether—it amplifies it. Stone that has stood for centuries suddenly remembers what it was built to do. To protect. To serve. To answer the call of Scarborne blood.

The walls pulse with silver light. The roof tiles rearrange themselves, forming patterns that hurt to look at directly. Even the trees in the garden lean inward, their branches reaching toward me like they're trying to shelter me from what's coming.

Seth screams.

Just once, sharp and sudden. Then there's nothing.

The weight on my arms vanishes. A sound like thunder echoes from where he was standing, but when I look, there's only empty space and a scorch mark burned into the stone.

I don't understand. Can't process what just happened through the chaos of power still tearing through me.

All I know is that suddenly I'm alone.

Phil throws up a shield, green light crackling around him as my power slams into it. But he's not fast enough, not strong enough. The Ether burns through his defenses like they're made of paper, sending him staggering backward with blood streaming from his nose.

"Impossible," he gasps, one hand pressed to his chest where the power scorched through. "You're untrained. You don't have the control for this kind of—"

The force builds again, tearing through what's left of his shield. The barrier buckles under the assault, cracks spreading across its surface like breaking ice. With a sound like thunder, it shatters completely.

The blast sends Phil flying. He hits the ground hard enough to crater the stone beneath him, his perfect suit reduced to smoking tatters. When he finally stops rolling, he's coughing up blood that steams where it touches the superheated ground.

For the first time since he arrived, Phil looks genuinely afraid.

But even wounded, even bleeding, his eyes still glitter with something like hunger. Like anticipation.

"Magnificent," he breathes, pushing himself up on his elbows. Blood runs from the corner of his mouth, but he's smiling. "All that fury, and not a drop of control. Do you see what you are now, Bree?"

He spits blood onto the cracked stone, his predatory grin widening despite the pain.

"You're not their queen. You're their executioner."

No.

I try to stand, to deny them, but my legs won't hold me. Everything hurts—my head, my chest, my hands. The taste of copper fills my mouth, and I can't tell if it's from the magic or from biting my tongue.

Around us, the destruction spreads. Cracks web through the courtyard. Windows lie in glittering fragments. The air still hums with residual power, making my skin crawl and my hair stand on end.

And in the center of it all, I kneel alone.

"You don't even know what you've done, do you?" Phil asks, and there's something almost gentle in his voice. Almost pitying. "Poor little Bree. So much power, so little understanding."

He gets to his feet with visible effort, straightening his ruined jacket like he's at a dinner party instead of the center of a magical catastrophe.

"But don't worry. Daddy will teach you. He's very good at teaching control."

Then he's gone, vanishing into shadow like he was never there at all.

The silence that follows feels like death.

I kneel in the center of destruction, surrounded by cracked stone and twisted metal and the charred remains of what used to be beautiful sanctuary grounds. The air tastes of ozone and burned magic, sharp and acrid in my throat.

The crowd is pressed against the far walls now, as distant from me as they can manage while still being in the same space. They're staring at me with expressions I've never seen before—not just fear, but revulsion. Horror. Like I'm something unnatural that's crawled up from the depths of hell.

And maybe I am.

Footsteps approach, but they're careful. Hesitant. Like the people making them aren't sure they want to get any closer.

The guys emerge from the crowd slowly, and I can see the exact moment they take in the full scope of what I've done. Gray's clothes are torn from his earlier transformation, dried blood still streaking his skin where the shift had torn through. His eyes are wild when they meet mine, but there's something else there too. Something that might be fear.

Of me.

Rhett smells of smoke and ash, heat still radiating from his skin in visible waves. His hands shake as he stares at the destruction, and I realize some of it came from him. His power, reacting to mine, adding to the chaos.

Wes looks like he might collapse. His face is pale, drained, and he won't meet my eyes. Can't meet my eyes, because he felt it all—my rage, my betrayal, my complete loss of control. The empathy that usually draws him to me must have been unbearable when I was like this.

Jace's knives are scattered across the ground, forgotten. He's staring at the place where Seth was standing, his usual cocky grin nowhere to be found. His face has gone gray, like he's seen something that will haunt him forever.

Theo approaches first, but even he stops several feet away. Like I'm something dangerous. Something that might explode again if he gets too close.

And maybe I will.

"Bree?" His voice sounds far away, careful and controlled in a way that makes my chest ache.

I look up at them through the haze of exhaustion and pain. Their faces are different somehow. Changed. There's something in their eyes that wasn't there before—not just concern or worry, but wariness. The kind of wariness you reserve for wild animals or unstable explosives.

They're afraid of me.

Really, truly afraid.

"I'm sorry," I whisper, my voice barely audible over the ringing in my ears. "I didn't mean—"

"Don't." Gray's voice cuts through the air, rough with something I can't identify. "Don't apologize."

But they're not coming closer. Even Wes, who usually can't help but reach for me when I'm hurting, stays frozen where he is. Like there's an invisible barrier between us now, built from fear and betrayal and the memory of what I'm capable of.

Nobody moves to help me up. Nobody offers comfort or reassurance or any of the gentle touches I've come to depend on.

They just stand there, staring at me like they've never seen me before.

Like they're not sure they want to.

Behind them, I catch sight of other faces in the crowd. Zira, her usual confidence replaced by something that looks like shock. Mairen, clutching her husband's arm with white knuckles. Even Stellan and Thane hang back, and these are men who've seen centuries of violence and power.

But they've never seen anything like this.

Never seen someone lose control so completely that they destroy everything around them without even meaning to.

I close my eyes and try to stop shaking, but the tremors won't fade. Neither will the taste of metal in my mouth, or the way the ground still hums with residual power beneath my knees, or the terrible certainty that I've crossed a line I can never uncross.

The Ether curls around my feet, subdued now but still threaded with those black veins. Still wrong. Still dangerous.

Still mine.

When I open my eyes again, the guys are still there. Still watching. Still afraid.

And somewhere in their faces, in the careful distance they're maintaining, I see the truth that Phil wanted me to understand.

I am exactly what he said I am.

Their executioner.

The only question now is whether they'll run before I hurt them too.

Chapter 24
STELLAN

Silence.

The kind that follows devastation, heavy and thick as smoke. I stand at the edge of the courtyard while the crowd presses against the sanctuary walls, their faces pale with terror and something deeper—the primal recognition that they've witnessed power beyond their comprehension.

The others hang back like she's become something radioactive. Gray's clothes are torn, dried blood streaking his skin where his earlier transformation left its mark. His eyes are wild when they find her, but there's wariness there now. Fear.

Rhett trembles despite the heat still radiating from his skin, his hands clenched at his sides like he's afraid to reach for her. Wes looks drained, hollow, his usual quiet intensity replaced by something that might be horror. Even Theo maintains his distance, brown eyes calculating but cautious.

Jace has gone completely still, his usual sharp grin nowhere to be found.

And Thane—Thane burns with fury, but it's impotent rage directed at everything except the girl kneeling in the center of destruction. Even he won't approach.

They see a weapon. A monster. Something that needs to be contained.

I see magnificence.

The courtyard is a masterpiece of controlled chaos. Where her silver Ether touched, flowers bloom from cracked stone—delicate, crystalline things that shouldn't exist but do anyway. Where the black threads reached, the ground has turned to obsidian glass that reflects nothing, drinking light like a hungry mouth.

The sanctuary itself responded to her call, stones singing with power they'd forgotten they possessed. Windows lie in glittering fragments, but the building stands stronger somehow. Like it finally remembered what it was built for.

This isn't destruction.

This is a coronation.

The woman in the center of it all kneels with her head bowed, silver and black Ether curling around her like a living crown. Her shoulders shake with what the others mistake for shame, but I can see the truth in the way the Ether moves—protective, reverent, claiming.

She whispers apologies, but the sanctuary doesn't accept them. The stones hum with approval, the very air crackling with recognition.

Something shifts in the spider-web cracks beneath her knees.

Shadows slink free from the obsidian glass—small, sleek creatures stitched from living darkness. One that might be a fox, another that could be a raven. Their forms shift and blur at the edges, too real to be illusions but too impossible to be natural.

The crowd gasps and stumbles backward, whispers of *corruption* and *taint* rippling through their ranks like poison.

But these creatures don't bare fangs. Don't attack or threaten.

They bow.

The shadow-fox lowers its head with liquid grace, dark eyes fixed on the woman who doesn't even notice its presence. The raven spreads wings made of night, dipping in a gesture of perfect reverence before dissolving back into the obsidian glass.

A third flickers at the edge of my vision—something serpentine and quick—just long enough to mirror the same motion before vanishing entirely.

My breath catches.

They think the black threads are rot spreading through silver light.

I see the truth.

The void doesn't bow to weakness. It doesn't acknowledge the broken or the corrupted. It recognizes only one thing: absolute authority.

These aren't signs of her fall. They're subjects paying homage to their queen.

While the others see infection, I'm witnessing expansion. Her power isn't being tainted—it's claiming new territory. The black threads aren't corruption bleeding into her Ether.

They're conquest.

The realization settles in my chest like warm honey, sweet and intoxicating. Around me, the crowd mutters about containment and control, about the danger she represents. They want to cage her, diminish her, make her small enough to feel safe.

They have no idea what they're looking at.

I take a step forward. Just one, deliberate and measured, letting my boots ring against the cracked stone. The sound cuts through the fearful whispers like a blade, and several heads turn my way.

But I'm not looking at them.

I'm looking at her.

Bree lifts her head slightly, green eyes finding mine across the devastation. There's pain there, confusion, the terrible weight of believing herself monstrous. But underneath—deeper, where she doesn't recognize it yet—there's something else.

Power that knows its own name.

I don't reach for her. Don't offer empty comfort or meaningless reassurance. I simply stand closer than anyone else dares, letting her feel my presence without intrusion.

Let her see that while the others recoil, I remain.

The shadow-fox appears again, just for a moment, padding silently across the obsidian glass to pause at her feet. It looks up at her with eyes like starlight before fading back into the cracks.

She doesn't notice. But I do.

In that moment, I understand exactly what she's becoming—and that sooner or later, she'll have to follow the shadows home.

Chapter 25
THANE

The silence stretches like a held breath, thick with fear and the metallic taste of raw power. I catalog the aftermath with practiced ease—cracked stone webbing outward from where she kneels, obsidian glass that doesn't belong here, flowers blooming impossibly from devastation. The sanctuary walls hum with awakened magic, and the crowd presses against them like they're the only thing standing between civilization and chaos.

Hundreds of Feeders and others hang back in various stages of terror. I can taste their panic on the air, sharp and acidic. They came here seeking salvation and witnessed what they believe is annihilation.

And at the center of it all, she kneels. Silver and black mist curls around her, power still crackling beneath her skin even as she whispers apologies to the cracked stone.

Stellan moves through the devastation with grace, stepping closer to her than anyone else dares. The others maintain their careful distance—Gray torn and bloodied from his earlier transformation, Rhett trembling despite the heat radiating from his skin, Wes pale and hollow-eyed. Even they fear what she's become.

What she's becoming.

Stellan pauses beside me, close enough that his voice carries only to my ears. When he speaks, each word lands like a blade between my ribs.

"You see a weapon. I see a queen."

The words hit something raw and furious in my chest. My jaw clenches, fangs pressing against my lower lip as I fight the urge to snarl at him. Queens don't leave scorch marks where their subjects used to stand. Queens don't thread void-touched darkness through their power like infection through silver light.

But even as the rage builds, Stellan's observation forces a crack in my certainty. Because he's not wrong about the way she commands the space around her, the way the ancient sanctuary responds to her presence like it's been waiting centuries for her return.

The way even the void-born creatures showed themselves bowed before dissolving back into shadow.

Their kind hasn't been seen in so long they were thought to be myth.

My mind races through calculations, probabilities, damage control. The community is fracturing. Feeders and others who came seeking hope now taste corruption in the air and whisper of curses. My people—the ones I've spent decades representing, protecting, keeping alive in a world that barely tolerates our existence.

But there's something else. Something that's been clawing at the edges of my control since we returned from that place of endless dark. The memory of her voice in the void, the way something else answered when she called out. The black threads that weren't part of her Ether but bled into it anyway, staining silver light with hungry shadows.

I felt it then. The presence that circled us like a predator, whispering things I couldn't quite hear but knew were poison. It touched her. Claimed pieces of her. Left its mark woven through her power like a signature of ownership.

That's what I'm really afraid of. Not her strength, but what's using it.

The crowd's whispers turn sharp, cutting through my thoughts like broken glass.

"She killed him."

"The void took him."

"She's cursed."

"Dangerous."

The word spreads like wildfire, panic rippling outward in visible waves. A cluster of Feeders surges forward, voices raised in accusation. Others drag them back, their own fear making them desperate for distance. Zira tries to raise her voice above the chaos, but she's drowned out by the growing hysteria.

Mairen clutches her son against her chest, tears streaming down her face as Kellan shouts for everyone to stop. But no one listens. The mob is seconds from igniting, and when it does, there won't be anything left to salvage.

I've seen this before. Watched communities tear themselves apart when fear overrides reason. Seen what happens when Feeders turn on each other, driven by hunger and desperation and the terrible certainty that survival requires sacrifice.

I won't watch it happen here. Not to her. Not to them.

The decision crystallizes without conscious thought.

"ENOUGH."

The word cracks across the courtyard like thunder, carrying centuries of authority and the unmistakable tone of an apex predator who's done tolerating insubordination. Every voice cuts off mid-syllable. Every movement freezes.

The silence that follows is absolute.

I step forward, positioning myself deliberately between Bree and the mob. Let them see exactly where I stand. Let them understand what it means to threaten something I've claimed as mine to protect.

"Seth is gone," I say, letting the words hang in the charged air. No point in pretending otherwise. They all saw the scorch mark, the empty space where a man used to be. "You witnessed his disappearance. You felt the power that tore through this place."

I pace slowly, forcing them to track my movement, to focus on my voice instead of their panic.

"But you also witnessed something else." My gaze sweeps across the crowd, noting which faces show confusion rather than terror. Those are the ones I can work with. "She did not strike him down. She did not drain his life or tear him apart. Something else took him. Through her."

The distinction matters. Has to matter. Because the alternative is watching them destroy the first real hope any of us have seen in generations.

"Phil walked away mostly unharmed," I continue, voice cutting through the uncertain murmurs. "The one who brought threats and violence to our sanctuary—he lives. But the man who stood close enough to touch her, who held her when she was vulnerable—he vanishes without a trace."

I let that sink in, watching understanding dawn on several faces.

"That was not her choice. That was not her power acting alone. Something older and hungrier reached through her to claim what it wanted. And if we turn on her now, if we abandon her to whatever force is hunting her, do you think it will be satisfied with just one?"

The crowd shifts restlessly, but the murderous edge has dulled to something more like wariness.

I gesture at the destruction around us—the cracked stone, the impossible flowers, the obsidian glass that drinks light like a hungry mouth. "Look at what woke when her blood called to it. Look at how this sacred ground answered her."

The sanctuary walls pulse with soft silver light, as if responding to my words. Ancient magic flows through stone and timber, power that's been sleeping for centuries suddenly vibrant and alive.

"That is not corruption," I say, letting my voice carry the full weight of my conviction. "That is dominion. This sanctuary recognizes her bloodline. It will protect us if we stand with her."

The political calculation is ruthless but necessary. Frame her as their shield instead of their weapon. Position her power as salvation rather than damnation. Give them something to rally behind instead of something to fear.

But even as I shape the narrative, even as I watch the crowd's hostility bleed into uncertain acceptance, my private thoughts burn with a different kind of fury.

She's not safe. Whatever touched her in that void-space, whatever whispered poison in her ear and threaded darkness through her light—it's still there. Still reaching for her. Still claiming pieces of what should be mine to protect.

The rage that coils in my chest isn't aimed at her. It's aimed at the presence that dared to mark her, to leave its signature woven through her power like a brand of ownership.

I will find what it is. I will hunt it through whatever realm it inhabits and tear it apart with my bare hands if necessary.

But not here. Not now. Not while she kneels in the center of devastation, trembling with exhaustion and shame, whispering apologies for power she never asked for.

The crowd has begun to settle, their panic subsiding into watchful quiet. Some still mutter among themselves, but the immediate threat of violence has passed. For now.

Across the courtyard, Stellan catches my eye. That faint, knowing smirk tugs at the corner of his mouth, like he's proud of the show I just gave. Like he knew exactly which buttons to press to get me to act.

I bare my fangs slightly but don't give him the satisfaction of a response.

Instead, I look back at her. Silver and black mist still curls around her feet, protective and possessive in equal measure. The others maintain their careful distance, but I can see the conflict in their faces. They want to comfort her, but they're afraid of what comfort might cost.

She's not just theirs anymore. Not just mine. She belongs to something that wants to claim her completely, to drag her into darkness and reshape her into its own image.

And I will not let it.

Whatever price that choice demands, whatever enemies it makes, whatever alliances it destroys—I will not let her be taken.

Not while I still have fangs to bare and blood left to spill.

Chapter 26
BREE

My knees are pressed into cracked stone. I can't get up. My head splits, hands shake, and my mouth tastes like metal and copper and something else I don't want to think about.

The crowd's gone quiet around me. Thane's voice still echoes off the walls from wherever he went, but all I can hear is the ringing in my ears and my own ragged breathing.

Phil was here. Phil found me. Found us. Found this place that was supposed to be safe and turned it into another nightmare. Just like the apartment. Just like everywhere else I've ever tried to exist.

But that's not even the worst part.

Seth's gone.

The thought keeps slamming into me like a fist to the chest. Over and over until I can't breathe around it. I keep seeing his face right before it happened. The way he looked at me when I begged him to let go. Not cruel. Not evil. Just... resigned. Like he was doing a job he didn't want to do but had to anyway.

It feels like I killed him.

My stomach lurches and I have to swallow hard to keep from throwing up right here on the broken stone. There's not even a body. Nothing to bury or mourn or apologize to. Just that burn mark a few feet away where a person used to be. Where Seth used to be.

I didn't even know I could do that. Make someone just… disappear. Like they never existed at all. Like the Ether reached out and decided they didn't deserve to take up space anymore.

What if it decides that about someone else? What if I lose control again and it's Gray this time, or Wes, or Rhett? What if I hurt the people I actually care about because I can't figure out how to stop being a weapon?

My chest tightens and spots dance across my vision. I can't breathe. Can't think. Can't do anything but kneel here and shake and taste metal and know that I'm exactly what Phil said I was.

Their executioner.

A shadow moves in the black glass under my knees.

I blink hard, trying to clear my vision, but it happens again. Like something's swimming underneath the surface, trying to break through.

A fox separates from the darkness.

It's small. Made of shadow that moves like smoke, but solid enough that I can see its eyes clearly. They burn like tiny stars in a face made of living darkness.

The crowd sucks in a collective breath. I hear someone whisper "void creature" and the fear spikes so sharp I can taste it.

I don't know what that means. Don't know what this thing is or why it's here. All I know is it came from the cracks my power made, and it's looking at me like it recognizes something.

But I'm not afraid.

I should be. Everything else about this whole nightmare should terrify me. But this little fox with its starry eyes doesn't feel dangerous. It feels…

familiar. Like recognizing something I've been waiting for without knowing it.

The fox tilts its head, watching me. Not afraid. Not angry. Not looking at me like I'm something that needs to be contained or destroyed or fixed.

Just curious.

Everyone's still staring at me. I can feel it. All those eyes waiting for me to explode again, to hurt someone else, to prove that letting me live was a mistake. Even the guys are keeping their distance. Even Gray, who's never been afraid of anything, hangs back like I might burn him if he gets too close. Only Stellan seems to have the nerve to step closer.

I reach out without thinking. My hand's shaking so bad I can barely control it, but I extend my fingers anyway. The fox could bite me. Could dissolve back into shadow. Could reject me like everyone else probably should.

Instead, it steps closer.

Its fur is impossibly soft under my fingertips. Cold like winter morning air, but solid. Real. Like touching starlight that somehow has texture and weight.

"You're not scared of me," I whisper.

The fox makes a sound deep in its throat. Not quite purring, but something close. Something that sounds almost like contentment.

And the Ether responds.

Silver light starts swirling up from the stone around my knees, black threads weaving through it like careful embroidery. Some of the silver light drifts toward the fox, drawn to it like metal to a magnet.

The fox doesn't flinch as the Ether touches its shadow-form. Instead, veins of silver begin tracing through its dark fur, not changing it but enhancing it. Making it more real, more solid, more *there*.

People gasp. Step back. I can practically feel them getting ready to run, to abandon this place and me along with it. But the fox just purrs deeper, leaning into both my touch and the silver light that's weaving itself into its being.

I'm so tired of being afraid of myself. So tired of apologizing for existing.

Maybe I no longer have to.

"Fix it," I tell the light, my voice cracking around the words. "Please. I don't want to break things anymore. I want to make them better."

The Ether listens.

It spreads out from where I'm kneeling in waves of silver shot through with black, and this time it doesn't destroy anything. This time it builds.

The cracks in the courtyard stone seal themselves, but not just sealed—stronger. The fractures fill with veins of silver that pulse like a heartbeat, like the sanctuary's learning to heal itself. The walls around us don't just repair—they grow. Stone flowing upward like water, adding height and thickness until they're more fortress than building. Protective. Defensible.

The shattered windows don't just piece themselves back together. They reform larger, clearer, with glass so pure it's almost invisible. But I can feel the wards woven into them, magical barriers that will keep out anything that means us harm.

Watchtowers emerge from the corners of the walls, graceful spirals of stone that reach toward the sky. Places to watch for threats. Places to see danger coming before it arrives.

The main gates thicken and strengthen, ancient wood becoming something that would take an army to breach. But they don't look forbidding. They look welcoming to anyone who comes in peace. Deadly to anyone who doesn't.

I don't fix everything, though. The flowers that grew from the cracks during my explosion—I leave those. They're beautiful. Crystalline petals that catch the light and throw it back in rainbows. They're proof that maybe I can make something good happen, even when everything goes wrong.

The fear in the crowd shifts, slowly, like ice beginning to thaw. I can hear whispered conversations, voices climbing from terror toward something else. Wonder, maybe. Or at least the possibility of it.

But there's something else. Something the Ether wants to build that I don't understand at first.

In the center of the courtyard, where the worst of the destruction was, a fountain begins to rise. Not water, but something else. Light that flows like liquid silver, pooling and cascading in patterns that hurt to look at directly but somehow comfort the soul.

At its base, words appear in the stone. Carved deep, filled with that same liquid light.

May Mirrors Weave The Way They're Meant

My throat closes up. The words don't make sense to me, but they feel important. Like a promise or a prayer carved in stone.

But the fox presses closer to my hand, and somehow I understand this isn't really about blame or forgiveness. Seth was caught between things bigger than him, forces he couldn't control. Whatever hold Phil had over him, whatever threats or promises or lies—Seth was as trapped as I was. Maybe more trapped, because at least I knew I was in a cage.

The memorial isn't for the spy who sold us out. It's for the person who deserved better than being trapped between impossible choices.

I blink, suddenly aware that I'm still kneeling by the fountain, one hand trailing in the liquid light. The courtyard comes back into focus around me—the strengthened walls, the watching crowd, the weight of all those eyes on me.

"She made it stronger," someone says behind me. Zira, I think. Her voice is soft with something like awe.

The fox nuzzles my palm once more, sparkling eyes meeting mine for a long moment. Then it starts fading, its edges blurring until it's just shadow again, then nothing.

"Don't go," I whisper, but it's already gone.

My hand feels empty where it was. Cold.

I force myself to stand up, using the fountain's edge for support. My legs shake like a newborn deer's, and I have to concentrate to keep from falling over, but I manage it.

The sanctuary looks... different. Better. Like a castle that could weather any storm. The walls rise high and strong around us, watchtowers keeping silent vigil. The gates stand ready to welcome friends and repel enemies.

It looks like a place that could keep us safe. All of us.

Seth's still gone. The fountain flows with its liquid light, beautiful and sad and permanent. Still proof of what happened, what I'm capable of.

But maybe... maybe if I can build things too, that counts for something.

Maybe I don't have to be just the person who breaks everything.

The Ether curls around me like a protective cloak, warm and comforting. Still silver shot through with black, but it doesn't feel wrong anymore. The black threads look like completion. Like the Ether needed both parts to be whole.

Like I need both parts to be whole.

I look up at the people gathered. The crowd is staring at all of it with expressions I can't read—fear and wonder and something that might eventually become trust.

They're still afraid of me. I can feel it. But they're not running.

And maybe that's enough to start with.

Maybe building something beautiful from the wreckage is enough.

That's what I thought I was doing with my life after all.

The Ether hums softly around me, patient and waiting. Ready for whatever comes next.

I'm still afraid of it. Still afraid of what I might do. But for the first time since this all began, I'm not afraid of myself.

Not entirely anyway.

Chapter 27
BREE

Standing beside the fountain, I feel the weight of every eye on me.

The liquid light still glows beneath the surface, Seth's memorial flowing in endless, beautiful loops. The fox is gone, faded back into shadow and memory, but its touch lingers on my palm. Around me, the crowd stays frozen—watching, waiting, trying to figure out what I am and what I might do next.

I catch a glimpse of myself in the fountain's surface and feel something twist in my chest. My reflection looks different. Not transformed. Just... clearer. Like I'm finally seeing myself instead of the smaller version I've been carrying around for as long as I can remember.

The person looking back at me doesn't seem like someone who would apologize for existing.

That darkness you fear in yourself? It's power.

Ethos's words echo in my mind—smooth as silk, and seductive in a way that does things to me I can't think about right now. Something about it feels wrong, but they settle into place anyway.

The power to take what you want instead of waiting to be given scraps.

The whisper carries a hunger that I'm not used to, but I can't bring myself to push it away.

I won't beg for honesty anymore. I'm not waiting for them to decide I'm worthy of trust, of truth, of being treated like I matter.

Because I deserve all of those things.

And more.

I turn toward the sanctuary, and when the building responds to my presence it feels like coming home. The stones hum softly beneath my feet. Carved symbols pulse with faint recognition as I pass.

When I step through the main hall, I stop.

There's something new. A raised dais of dark stone has emerged from the floor at the far end—not quite a throne room, but the beginning of one. The platform is elegant, understated, like the sanctuary is testing an idea. Seeing if I'll accept what it's offering.

My breath catches. The sight should unnerve me. Should send me running.

Instead, it feels like coming home.

But the guys—

They hang back like I might shatter if they get too close.

Gray keeps his distance, storm-colored eyes tracking my movement with something between hunger and wariness. Rhett's hands twitch at his sides like he wants to reach for me but doesn't dare. Even Jace, who's never met a boundary he couldn't charm his way across, stays carefully out of arm's reach.

The contrast should hurt. It did hurt, before the fountain. Before Seth. Before everything changed.

Before the truth of everything became clear in my head.

Now it just makes something sharp and bright unfurl behind my ribs. *If they're afraid of me, maybe they should be.*

I pause just inside the sanctuary's main hall, and the weight of their attention feels like something I can use. The Ether swirls around my feet, silver shot through with those black threads that everyone keeps pretending they don't see.

"So," I say, and my voice carries in a way it never has before. Like it knows exactly where it belongs. "Are you going to tell me what you've been hiding, or should I guess?"

The silence that follows feels different than their usual careful quiet. This one has weight to it.

Rhett shifts his weight, jaw ticking. "Bree—"

"You left me kneeling in that courtyard," I continue, cutting him off. The words taste like power and betrayal at the same time. "While they called me dangerous. While Phil's threats hung over these people. And you all just... watched."

I look at each of them, really look, and it's like seeing them for the first time. Gray's hunger beneath that careful mask. Rhett's heat making the air shimmer between us, but his hands staying carefully at his sides. Theo's guilt written across his face in lines I know how to read now. Wes near the doorway, lips parted like he wants to speak but can't quite find the words.

Thane won't even look at me directly. Like he's afraid of what he'll see reflected back.

Only Stellan steps closer instead of back, just like he did in the courtyard. His eyes hold approval, sharp and unflinching—like he sees what I'm becoming and dares the others to admit it.

"You want me when I'm small," I say, taking a step forward. Several of them take a step back, and that tells me everything I need to know. "When

I'm manageable. When I need saving. But when I'm real—when I'm all of it—you can't handle it."

"That's not—" Rhett starts, heat shimmering around his shoulders.

"Isn't it?"

The question hangs there, and I can see the answer written across their faces. The way they want to reach for me but don't. The way desire wars with something that looks a lot like fear.

I'm done being the one who reaches first.

"You're afraid," I say, and the observation settles into place like a key turning in a lock. "All of you. Except—" My gaze finds Stellan, who still hasn't stepped back. "Thank you."

The words create a crack swear I can see. Thane's jaw ticks, and the others exchange looks that feel loaded with something sharp. Stellan's small smile feels like drawing a line in the sand.

When nobody else speaks, I feel something that might be disappointment, if disappointment could cut like this.

Jace shifts his weight, blades catching the light. His face closes off before he speaks. "We found something," he says, voice tight in a way I haven't heard before. "In your apartment. Back before any of this started. Cameras."

The word stings and for a moment, everything goes quiet. My power dims—silver threads flickering like candles in a sudden breeze. I'm back in that tiny space, changing clothes, showering, crying myself to sleep while someone *watched*. While someone recorded every private moment and probably shared them with—

"You've known." My voice comes out flat, deadly quiet. "For how long?"

"Bree—"

"How. Long."

The silence stretches until I think it might snap and cut us all to pieces.

"Since the night Jace and Theo moved you out," Gray finally says, the admission torn from somewhere deep in his chest. "Since Jace moved you out."

Since the beginning. They've known since the *beginning* that Phil violated my privacy in the most intimate way possible, and they decided I couldn't handle the truth. They looked at me—broken, terrified, barely holding myself together—and chose to manage me instead of trusting me.

The betrayal feels different this time. Not like drowning, but like lightning. Sharp and clean and illuminating.

"You kept me powerless," I say, and my voice doesn't shake. "You made decisions about my life, my safety, my right to know what was happening to me. And you called it protection."

"We were trying to keep you safe," Rhett says, but there's something careful in his voice. Like he's testing words before he speaks them. "Phil is—"

"Don't." The word stops him cold. "Don't stand there and tell me what Phil is after everything you've hidden."

"You're not yourself," Thane says, stepping forward with that measured control he wears like armor.

"Are you kidding me right now?" I turn on him, and something hot and jagged unfurls in my chest. "You don't know who I am. Not after you—"

I cut myself off, but we both know what I'm not saying. What I can't say with everyone listening.

After you couldn't protect me in the Void. After you let something else touch my mind while you just stood there.

Thane goes very still, and I watch him realize exactly what I'm referring to. What I'm choosing not to say out loud.

"It wasn't like that," Rhett says, still trying to defend them. "We were trying to—"

"To what?" I interrupt, and this time I'm the one moving closer. He flinches—actually flinches—from the Ether writhing around me. "To keep me compliant? To make sure I stayed grateful and quiet while you handled the big scary world for me?"

His mouth opens, closes. No words come out.

"Touch me," I say.

The command stops everyone cold.

"You want to protect me so badly. You want to make decisions for me, keep secrets from me, treat me like I'm made of glass. So touch me." I spread my arms wide, Ether crackling between my fingers like miniature lightning. "Show me that you're not afraid."

Wes takes half a step forward, fingers reaching before he catches himself and stops. The aborted motion hurts worse than if he'd never moved at all. Like a door slammed just as I reached for it.

But Stellan moves closer, elegant and unafraid, while the others flinch away. The contrast draws sharp lines between them—those who fear what I'm becoming, and the one who sees it as something else.

"Stellan." Thane's voice carries a warning, but Stellan ignores it completely.

He steps close enough that I can feel the warmth of him, leans down until his lips brush my ear. "You're magnificent," he whispers, and his voice does something to my pulse that I wasn't expecting.

Then he presses a soft kiss to my cheek before pulling away, gray eyes holding mine for a heartbeat. The Ether around me actually settles at his touch, silver threads calming instead of lashing. He winks—actually winks—and walks back to stand with the others like he didn't just prove every single one of their fears wrong.

The gesture hits me harder than it should. Not because of the kiss, but because of what it means. He touched me. Willingly. Without fear.

While the others stand there with want in their eyes, but fear still chains them where they stand.

The air grows thick with want and fear and something that tastes like the beginning of an ending.

"That's what I thought."

I lower my arms, and it feels like closing a book.

"I'm not asking for your trust anymore," I tell them, and the words feel like stepping into something I should have claimed a long time ago. "You lost that chance. But here's the thing—I don't need it. I don't need permission."

The sanctuary responds like it's been waiting for me to say exactly that. Walls hum with approval. Doors that were closed swing open. Pathways become clear and bright.

Wes makes a small sound. "Bree, please—"

"Please what? Please go back to being small? Please pretend I don't see how you all step back when my power shows? Please keep letting you decide what's best for me?"

I shake my head, and it feels like shaking off something that never fit right anyway.

"You'll have to decide if you can handle all of me," I tell them, already moving toward the deeper corridors where I know the sanctuary's heart is waiting. "Because I won't go back to being managed. I won't go back to being less."

The black threads in my Ether pulse once, and I taste something that isn't mine—approval, pride, hunger that goes deeper than want.

Good, something whispers where only I can hear it, and the voice definitely isn't mine. *Let them see what you really are.*

The thought should disturb me more than it does.

"You wanted to keep me small," I say over my shoulder as I walk away from them. "But I was never meant to be small."

My footsteps echo in the corridor, and I don't look back to see if they follow.

Chapter 28
THEO

I've been lying here for three hours, staring at the ceiling of my bedroom while guilt gnaws at my chest like something alive. Every time I close my eyes, I see Bree's face from yesterday—the careful blankness in her green eyes when I finally cornered her in the hallway, the way she said *"It's fine, Theo. Really"* like she was reading from a script.

It's not fine. Nothing about this is fine.

I broke something between us when the truth about Phil came out. When she realized we'd all been keeping secrets, that we'd decided together she couldn't handle the truth. When she looked at each of us like we'd chosen to betray her instead of protect her. The memory makes me want to punch something—preferably myself.

Two days of watching her avoid eye contact. Two days of feeling like I've lost her trust right when she needs me. Two days of knowing we all failed her when it mattered most.

And two days of visions that keep getting worse.

That's the part that's eating at me. Ever since Phil showed up and everything went to hell, my gift has been showing me fragments that feel darker, more fractured. Like the future itself is responding to the cracks we put in her trust. We've always been a unit, us and Bree. Even with the recent additions to our group, it was still Bree at our core and us circling around her—protecting, caring, keeping her safe. Now all she sees when she looks at us, looks at me, is someone she can no longer trust.

And the visions reflect that. Each one worse than the last, showing possibilities that make my chest tight with dread.

The sanctuary hums; tonight it feels like a living thing tugging at my skull. I can feel it pulling at the edges of my consciousness, the way it always does when visions want to come.

I roll over, pressing my face into the pillow. "No," I mutter into the fabric. "Not tonight."

But the pull intensifies, that familiar electric tingle behind my eyes that means my gift won't be ignored. The Ether in this place amplifies everything—Bree's power, our bonds, and apparently my ability to see things I don't want to see.

The vision takes me before I can fight it.

Flash—

Bree in chains, silver and delicate but binding. Her head bowed, Ether pooling at her feet like spilled mercury. She's not fighting them. Just... accepting.

Flash—

Bree before a mirror, hand pressed to glass. Dark hair, familiar build, but when she turns—her eyes hold a certainty I've never seen before. Confident where she usually hesitates.

Flash—

Bree surrounded by faces I can't quite focus on, confusion written across her features. She reaches for something—someone—but her hands pass through empty air.

Flash—

Bree standing before a kneeling crowd. They look at her like she's every-thing they've been waiting for. She accepts their worship like it's natural, earned, right.

Flash—

Black Ether curling around Bree's ankles, drawing her in. Her face flick-ers between expressions—vulnerable one moment, commanding the next.

Flash—

A bed, soft murmurs in the darkness. Rhett's face in gentle light, watch-ing Bree with adoration I've never seen from him. She moves with fluid certainty that makes my chest tight.

Flash—

Bree in the darkness, dirty and broken with tears streaking down her cheeks as she embraces...

Flash—

Bree leaning close; a wordless warmth grazes my skin. I want to follow, and I don't know why.

The fragments come faster, overlapping and contradicting each other. Different versions of Bree—wounded and whole, uncertain and com-manding—both equally real, both equally impossible. They flicker like competing flames, each image warring with the next.

Then they shatter.

I jolt back into myself with a gasp that tears from my throat like a sob. My heart pounds against my ribs, head splitting from the effort of processing visions that make no sense. Sweat sticks my shirt to my chest despite the cool night air.

What the hell was that?

I sit up, gripping the edge of my bed until my knuckles go white. The fragments feel important—prophetic—but I can't piece them together into anything coherent. Was I seeing Bree's future? Someone else's? Multiple possibilities bleeding together?

And why did some of those images feel so wrong? Like looking at Bree in moments that didn't match who she is?

My door creaks open without a knock.

"You look like you saw a ghost."

Jace leans against the doorframe, spinning a blade between his fingers with casualness that suits him. His golden hair is mussed like he just woke up, but his green eyes are sharp.

"Drop it," I snap, though the words come out rougher than I intended.

He raises an eyebrow, unbothered by my tone. "Well, that's convincing. Nothing says 'I'm fine' like snarling at concerned friends." The blade vanishes up his sleeve with a practiced flick. "Wanna try that again?"

I drag both hands through my hair, trying to center myself. The vision fragments still pulse behind my eyes like afterimages, making it hard to focus on the present.

"Just a nightmare," I lie.

"Right." Jace pushes off the doorframe and steps into my room uninvited, golden eyes scanning my face in a way that makes me uncomfortable. "And I'm the Queen of England. Come on, Theo. I've seen you after regular nightmares. This is different."

He's not wrong. Jace might hide behind humor and irreverence, but he notices everything. It's what makes him dangerous with those knives of his—and what makes him impossible to lie to when he's actually paying attention.

"It's nothing I can explain," I say finally. "Just... fragments. Images that don't make sense."

"About Bree?"

The question hits something in my chest. "Maybe. I don't know." I look up at him, weighing how much to share. "Have you noticed anything... different about her lately?"

"You mean besides the fact that she's been avoiding all of us like the plague?" Jace's mouth quirks in what might be sympathy. "Or the way her Ether looks darker than it used to?"

That stops me cold. "You've seen it too?"

"The black threads?" He shrugs, but his casual tone doesn't match the sharpness in his eyes. "Hard to miss. Rhett thinks it's trauma from the Void thing. Wes thinks it's her power evolving. Thane won't talk about it, even though he was there." His voice drops slightly. "What do you think it is?"

I stare at him, pieces clicking together in my head. The vision fragments, the black threads in Bree's Ether, the way she's been different since she came back. Not just distant—changed in subtle ways that make my instincts scream.

"I think," I say slowly, "that something's coming. Something that's going to change everything."

"Well." Jace's grin turns sharp, but there's genuine concern underneath it. "That's not ominous at all."

He moves toward the door, then pauses on the threshold. "For what it's worth? Whatever you saw, whatever's coming—we'll handle it. For Bree."

Then he's gone, leaving me alone with fragments that feel like prophecy and a growing certainty that I've seen something I wasn't supposed to.

Two versions of Bree. One broken, one whole. One uncertain, one commanding.

Both equally real.

Both impossible.

I close my eyes and let my head fall back against the wall.

If that's what's coming... how do I tell her without breaking her again?

Chapter 29
BREE

The world folds like a page and I'm somewhere else.

No transition, no falling asleep. One moment I'm lying in my bed, the next I'm standing in a room made of mirrors and golden light that smells like sweat and honey.

The chamber stretches impossibly wide, each surface reflecting warmth that makes the air shimmer. This isn't the sanctuary—definitely not anywhere I recognize. But it feels like home in a way that makes my chest tight.

"You came back."

I turn toward the voice and see her. The woman from before. Dark hair, green eyes that actually sparkle instead of carrying all the weight mine do. She looks like me, but... better. Like someone took all my broken pieces and put them back together the right way.

Riley.

"I've been waiting," she says, and even her voice sounds more confident than mine ever has. "They're here too."

Gray appears at my left, shoulders relaxed for once instead of tensed for the next disaster. His thumbs circle my cheek, slow as worship. "Let me keep this," he breathes, and the word feels like a promise.

Rhett's hand finds the small of my back, protective warmth turned intimate. "You're mine to keep," he says like a vow, voice low and certain in a way that makes heat pool in my stomach.

Wes moves to my right, none of that careful hunger in his eyes that makes him hold back. His palm settles over my heart. "Here. I belong here," he says, steady as a promise, and for once his touch doesn't make him flinch.

Jace laughs, soft and edged with ownership. "Don't go anywhere. Not on my watch," he murmurs, fingers tracing the line of my jaw like he's memorizing it.

Theo steps closer, none of the guilt that's been weighing down his words lately. "No more distance," he says, hands anchoring me like salvation. "No more walking on eggshells."

And Thane—God, Thane. He leans against one of the mirrors with his usual elegant composure, but there's no coldness in his silver eyes. His gaze is hungry and soft at the same time, watching me like I'm something worth keeping instead of something that might break his careful control.

Even Stellan is here, and his touch barely brushes my shoulder, but there's approval in the stillness. That polite distance he always maintains has melted into something warmer, more present.

This is what I've been craving. What I've been missing since everything went to hell. To be cherished instead of managed, claimed instead of protected from afar.

Riley watches from beside one of the mirrors, smiling like she knows a secret. "This is how it should be," she says softly. "This is what you deserve."

Gray's grip on my face becomes firmer, more possessive. "No more secrets," he promises, and the relief that floods through me is so intense it's almost painful.

Rhett pulls me back against his chest, and I can feel the heat radiating from him like being wrapped in fire. "All ours," he murmurs against my ear, voice rough with want.

Thane pushes off from the mirror, moving with that predatory grace he has. "Mine to protect," he says, voice carrying that dangerous edge I've learned to crave. "Mine to feed from. Mine to keep safe."

Stellan's fingers tangle in my hair, touch light but possessive. "You don't need anyone else," he whispers, breath warm against my neck. "We're enough. We're everything."

The golden warmth wraps around me, but it's more intense now. Heavier. Like being claimed by all of them at once, and I want to drown in it.

But Riley's reflection starts to waver, and she's smiling wider now. "You could have him too," she says, voice growing distant but pleased. "Why settle for just them?"

The golden light fractures, pulling Riley into darkness that swallows her whole. The guys fade with her, but not before I see something flicker in their eyes—a hunger that goes deeper than want, darker than love.

Then I'm alone in the dark, but it's not empty.

It's full of him.

He steps out of the dark like a sin I've been rehearsing for.

"Hello, little queen."

The voice slides through me like warm honey, and I know exactly who he is. The sound of it is carved into my bones, whispered in my dreams, threaded through every moment I've reached for more than I was offered.

"Ethos," I breathe, and saying his name feels like coming home.

Beautiful doesn't even begin to cover it. Dark hair that catches light that doesn't exist, pale skin that seems to glow from within. When he looks at me, those silver-black eyes hold recognition, like he's been watching me my whole life.

"You have been calling," he says, moving closer. Not an accusation—a certainty. Like he's been waiting for this moment as long as I have.

"I haven't—"

"Haven't you?" His fingers brush my wrist, and silver chains shimmer into existence. Not rough metal, but something that looks like captured moonlight and cool against my skin. "Every time you take what you want instead of waiting to be given scraps. Every time you demand instead of asking. You've been becoming who you were meant to, becoming mine."

The chains feel like silk, beautiful and binding. "This is what you crave," he says, voice dropping to that intimate tone that makes my skin burn. "Not their careful touches, their held-back hunger. You want to be consumed."

His lips brush my throat, and I gasp as more chains appear, winding around my ankles, my waist. Each one sends pleasure shooting through me, dark and addictive.

"Surrender is not loss," he murmurs against my neck. "It is choosing who holds you."

I want to argue, but his touch is setting me on fire. The chains tighten in rhythm with his movements, and I realize they're not just restraining me—they're bringing us together, closer than I've ever been with anyone.

"Give me your light," he whispers as my Ether flows between us in steady pulses. With each one, he grows more solid, more present, more real.

"That's it," he encourages, voice rough with hunger. "Give me what you want me to take."

The Ether weaves between us like silk, and instead of feeling drained, I feel... connected. Like every pulse of power that passes between us proves how much we need each other.

"You were made for this—bright, burning, given wholly," he murmurs against my lips. The kiss is everything—demanding, sure, unafraid. When his teeth graze my bottom lip, I gasp, and more silver light weaves between us.

The chains pull tighter, drawing more Ether, and the pleasure blurs with something darker. Something that makes the golden warmth from before feel pale and empty.

"More," I hear myself whisper, and I'm not sure if I mean his touch or the strange sensations or both.

He smiles against my throat, fangs scraping skin. "Mine," he breathes. Not a want, a fact. "You were made to be taken."

The chains are bright now, fed by the energy flowing between us until they're almost too beautiful to look at. And with every pulse that connects us, I feel more wanted, more needed, more whole than I ever have.

But something shifts. The pleasure frays at the edges—too sharp, too fast. The chains tighten like they've stopped listening to me, pulling harder than I meant them to.

"More," I hear myself whisper again, but my voice sounds strange. Distant.

He smiles against my throat, fangs grazing skin. "There you are," he croons, and the certainty in his voice should feel like safety. Instead, my chest flutters with something unfamiliar.

The mirrors catch my face—but the eyes staring back aren't mine. Too bright. Too silver. A stranger wearing my smile.

"Perfect," he says, voice soft as silk, and it sounds less like accusation and more like destiny.

But destiny feels heavier than I expected.

The chains pulse again, drawing more Ether, and this time the sensation makes me gasp. Not entirely from pleasure. A hollowness grows with each pull, spreading through my chest like cold water.

"That's enough," I whisper, but the words feel weak.

He doesn't stop. His touch becomes more insistent, more possessive. "Don't think," he murmurs. "Just feel. Just give."

The chamber around us tilts, and in the mirrors I catch glimpses of myself—pale, drained, while silver light mixed with black flows from me in streams that hurt and please at the same time.

My reflection smiles back at me with eyes that aren't quite mine anymore.

"Something's wrong," I whisper, though even as the words slip free I can't explain them. Everything feels perfect—too perfect—so why does my chest feel tight, like I'm already drowning?

"Nothing is wrong," he says gently, thumb stroking over my cheek. "This is exactly what you wanted."

And it is. Isn't it?

The thought should comfort me, but it doesn't.

The chains pulse one more time, harder, and my scream tears through whatever space we're in.

I jolt awake gasping, sheets soaked with sweat. My wrists ache like they're still bound, and I can taste copper and something older than grief in my mouth.My hands won't stop shaking. My chest feels too tight, my breath too shallow.

It was good. It was everything I wanted.

So why does my body feel like it just survived something terrible?

Footsteps thunder down the hallway. My door crashes open, and they pour in.

"Bree," Theo breathes, reaching for me first, fingers hovering before he settles his hand on my shoulder. "You're here. You're safe," he says, voice thick with relief, and I can see the fear that's been eating at him.

Rhett moves to my other side, scanning me for injuries. "What happened? You screamed."

Gray appears at the foot of my bed, sharp eyes taking in my shaking hands, the sweat-soaked sheets. "Talk to me," he says, steady despite the concern written across his face. "Are you okay?"

"Nightmare," Jace says, but there's no dismissal in his voice. Just worry. "Must have been a hell of one."

Wes hovers near the door, dark eyes tracking the black mist still curling around me. His expression is careful, like he's trying not to crowd me but doesn't want to leave either.

Thane appears in the doorway behind them, silver eyes sharp and assessing. Stellan follows, quiet and watchful.

They're all here. All worried. All looking at me like I matter, like my pain matters.

But they don't feel like Riley's men. Don't move with that possessive certainty, that unquestioning adoration. They're careful with me. Gentle. Like they're afraid of pushing too hard.

Like they think I might break.

I try to speak, to explain, but all that comes out is a whisper that feels torn from my chest:

"Ethos."

The name hangs in the air, foreign and heavy. I watch their faces change—confusion replacing concern.

Stellan goes completely still. "Where did you hear that name?" His voice is carefully controlled, but I catch the edge underneath.

"Who's Ethos?" Gray asks quietly.

Thane steps into the room, recognition flickering in his silver eyes. "The voice," he says slowly. "From the Void. That was his name?"

I nod, unable to find words.

"What voice?" Rhett demands, looking between us with growing alarm.

"There was something else there with us," Thane explains, his voice carefully controlled even as his silver eyes track Stellan's reaction. "Something that spoke. Tried to..." He stops, jaw tightening as he looks at me. "Something that wants her."

Stellan's face drains of color and he takes a sharp step back, like the words themselves are a physical blow. "No," he breathes, voice raw with something that might be terror. "Not her. He can't—" He cuts himself off, running a hand through his hair with shaking fingers.

But I can't answer. Can't explain how it felt more real than the room around me, or how part of me is already missing the certainty of those chains.

The silence stretches between us, heavy with dread and the lingering feeling of something dark.

And all I can think about is him.

Chapter 30
RHETT

I can't get the sound of her scream out of my head.

It's been echoing in my skull for an hour — raw, terrified, squeezing my chest. The way she looked at me with wide eyes, sheets soaked with sweat, black mist pouring off her like fire turned inside out. The way her hands shook when she whispered that name.

Ethos.

My fire answers the memory, heat prickling under my skin like a warning. I should have been faster. Should have reached her before whatever the hell that was finished with her. Should have done something other than stand there useless while she looked at us like we were strangers.

She's upstairs now. Gray said a bath might help, so he got it ready for her and gave her space. For some reason it makes her absence cut sharper, the betrayal sting worse.

Because that's what this is, isn't it? Betrayal. Not just from Thane — his secrets about Phil cut deep enough — but from her. From Bree.

The others look as wrecked as I feel. Jace paces near the window, looking out like he might find answers there. Gray sits rigid in his chair, jaw locked. Wes hovers by the doorway like he wants to bolt, dark eyes tracking the hall. Theo looks haunted, brown eyes distant in that way they get when he's seeing things the rest of us can't.

Thane leans against the far wall, silver eyes unreadable. Stellan stands beside him, silent and watchful.

We're all here, shaken and looking for answers.

"Somebody explain who the hell Ethos is — before I start throwing knives," Jace snaps, stopping his pacing to glare at the room. His usual humor is gone, replaced by sharp-edged frustration.

All eyes turn to Thane. His silver gaze flicks between us, and for a moment his mask slips completely.

"She heard him," Thane says quietly. "In the Void. He spoke to her — tried to tempt her with something." His jaw tightens. "He only spoke to me briefly. I couldn't hear what he was saying to her, only that she was hearing something. Someone."

The admission hangs heavy in the air.

"And we didn't tell you," he finishes.

Silence stretches, heavy with implication.

"You both knew," Wes says quietly, his voice cutting like a whip. "And you kept it from us."

His hurt is raw. Mine is too. I want to protect her — want to be the one who carries the weight for her — and instead I'm learning she carried this alone.

"Would knowing have changed anything?" Thane asks, calm and sharp. "Would telling you a name have stopped him? Would you rather she carried your fear on top of her own?"

I see red.

Heat lashes through the room. Flames lick under my skin as my fist splinters the chair arm. I stand, chest burning.

"You don't get to decide for us!" The words tear out of me. "Not you, not her, not anyone. We're supposed to share this. Protect each other. You kept us out — you made us weak. You made her weak."

"And where is she now?" I continue, the betrayal cutting. "Hiding upstairs because she wouldn't trust us enough to tell us what was hunting her. Because she thought we couldn't handle it."

"It wasn't like that," Thane says sharply. "But you're proving my point."

The words hit like a slap. I take a breath, the fire guttering as I realize he's right. My anger, my hurt - it's exactly what Bree was trying to protect us from. Protect herself from.

"Ethos isn't a name you speak lightly," Stellan says quietly. There's weight in his voice that makes everyone turn.

"You know him?" Gray asks.

Stellan's expression darkens. "I ended up there once. The Void." His voice is barely above a whisper. "By accident. It's a twisted, insidious place that feeds on your worst impulses." He takes a breath, heavy with something like shame. "I made a deal with Ethos to make it back."

The silence that follows is deafening. Everyone stares at Stellan like they're seeing him for the first time.

"Is he more dangerous to us, to Bree than the Council?" Jace asks, incredulous.

Stellan's laugh is bitter. "The Council wants control. Ethos wants to remake the realms in his image and make you believe it was your choice." His eyes find the hall again. "If he's coming for her, we're in worse trouble than you realize."

The words settle like a shroud. Ethos is more than a voice.

"Anyone else have secrets they want to share?" Gray asks, razor-sharp. "Because now seems like a good time to get everything out in the open."

Silence hangs heavy. Everyone is doing mental math, weighing what they know against what they've kept.

Theo runs both hands through his hair. "Actually... there's something else. Something Seth and I found a while back."

My blood chills. "What kind of something?"

"Ruins," Theo says quietly. "Old ones. Hidden in the sanctuary grounds. They responded to my touch — like they were waiting." He meets my eyes. "There's a chamber underneath. Stairs that lead down. I found pieces of a mirror at the top of the stairs."

"Mirrors?" Thane's voice is flat now, sharp enough to make my skin crawl.

Theo nods. "Broken mirror pieces. Shattered." His voice gets quieter. "But it felt like Bree. Like power. She needs to see it."

The room goes dead silent. Even the sanctuary seems to hold its breath.

"You didn't think to mention this sooner?" Jace asks, deadly quiet.

"I was going to," Theo snaps, defensive. "But there's always something — chaos, attacks, crises —" He gestures helplessly.

The heat in my chest gutters, replaced by cold dread. Theo's right. The betrayal stings, but none of that matters if we lose her.

"It doesn't matter why he didn't tell us," I say, the irony not lost on me. "What matters is we have a place to start looking."

The anger burns hot and sharp, but deeper than that is something unshakable: I will keep her safe.

Even if she won't let me.

Even if she didn't trust me enough to tell me that something's hunting her.

The silence stretches, full of fractured trust and questions no one can answer. Outside, the sanctuary hums with old power, but it feels thin — like these walls might not be enough.

I swore I'd never fail her again. But if she keeps locking me out, how the hell am I supposed to protect her?

The question hangs between us, raw and unanswered. One thing is clear — whatever comes next, we can't face it divided.

We have to put the pieces back together — fast — or Ethos will tear us apart.

"Hey guys," Wes says quietly, his voice cutting through the heavy silence. "Does Bree even realize she's being hunted?"

Fuck.

Chapter 31
JACE

"Why do we have to do this again?"

Bree's voice is muffled by the pillow she's got pressed over her face, but the frustration comes through loud and clear. It's been two days of this — Bree pretending everything is fine when it definitely is not.

I lean against her doorframe, arms crossed, watching her burrow deeper into the covers like she can disappear if she tries hard enough. Even like this — hair a mess, face hidden, radiating stubborn defiance — she's beautiful. Makes me want to crawl into that bed and kiss her until I'm all she can think about.

But that's not what she needs right now.

"Because you've stayed in bed avoiding us long enough," I say, keeping my voice light but firm. "It's time to face this. Together."

"I'm not avoiding anything." The pillow muffles her words, but I catch the defensive edge.

"Right. And I'm not devastatingly handsome." I push off the doorframe and walk over to sit on the edge of her bed. The mattress dips under my weight, and she rolls slightly toward me despite herself. "Look, I know we told you yesterday about Ethos hunting—"

"Stop." Bree says clearly exasperated even through the pillow. "Just stop."

"Bree—"

"You don't know what you're talking about," she snaps, sitting up abruptly. "I'm fine."

She finally pulls the pillow away from her face, and I have to bite back a wince. Dark circles under her eyes, hair a tangled mess, that stubborn set to her jaw that means she's about to dig in deeper.

"You suck," she mutters.

"Look, I get it." I reach over and tug gently at a strand of her hair until she looks at me. "The whole ruins thing is scary as hell, it's probably like every horror movie rolled into one."

Her eyes flick away. "It's not that."

"Then what is it?"

She's quiet for so long I think she's not going to answer. When she finally speaks, her voice is small. "What if I make it worse? What if whatever's down there is better off staying buried?"

And there it is. The real fear. Not of what she might find, but of what she might unleash.

"Bree." I wait until she meets my eyes again. "You know what's worse than facing whatever's down there?"

"What?"

"Letting Ethos keep whispering in your ear while you hide up here." Her face goes pale, but I press on. "That thing — whatever he is — he's counting on you being too scared to act. He wants you isolated, second-guessing yourself."

"You don't understand—"

"I understand that you screamed his name in your sleep last night," I say quietly. "I understand that there's something hunting you, and sitting here pretending it's not happening isn't going to make it go away."

She flinches like I've slapped her, but I can see the fight starting to come back into her eyes. Good. Angry Bree is better than defeated Bree.

"Besides," I add, grinning at her, "I promise I'll make we-made-it-out-alive pancakes when we get back."

Despite everything, her mouth twitches. "We-made-it-out-alive pancakes?"

"Only the finest. With enough butter to stop your heart and syrup that costs more than most people's rent." I lean closer, mock-serious. "But only if you get your ass out of this bed and come face whatever ancient horror is waiting for us."

She stares at me for a long moment, and I can practically see the war happening behind her eyes. Fear versus determination. The urge to hide versus the need to act.

Finally, she sighs and throws the covers back. "You're manipulative, you know that?"

"I prefer 'strategically motivating,'" I say, standing up and offering her my hand. "Come on. The others are waiting."

She takes my hand and lets me pull her to her feet. She's wearing one of Gray's hoodies — the oversized black one that makes her look even smaller than she is — and her hair is definitely going to need some work before we go anywhere.

"How long do I have to get ready?" she asks, already moving toward her bathroom.

"Twenty minutes. And Bree?" I wait until she turns back to look at me. "For what it's worth, I don't think you're going to make anything worse. I think you're going to make it right."

She doesn't answer, but something in her expression softens just a little. It's not much, but hopefully it's enough.

I head for the door, pausing in the threshold. "Oh, and sweetheart? Brush your hair. You look like you've been fighting with a hedge."

Something hits the door just as I duck out, and I can hear her muttering curses behind me. But she's moving, and that's what matters.

Now I just have to convince the others that dragging our girl into ancient ruins filled with mysterious mirrors is a good idea.

Piece of cake.

Twenty minutes later, we're gathered in the sanctuary's main room, and the tension is so thick you could cut it with one of my knives. Bree's cleaned up — hair brushed, face washed, wearing actual clothes instead of stolen hoodies — but she's still got that deer-in-headlights look that makes me want to wrap her in bubble wrap.

The others aren't much better. Rhett's jaw is set like he's preparing for battle. Gray keeps checking and rechecking his gear with the kind of obsessive precision that means he's nervous. Wes hovers near Bree like a satellite, drawn to her orbit but still afraid to get too close even though we all know what happened between them. Theo looks like he hasn't slept since Bree's nightmare, dark circles under his eyes making him look haunted.

Even Thane and Stellan seem on edge, though they're better at hiding it.

"Everyone ready?" I ask, shouldering my pack. The knives at my belt feel reassuring, their familiar weight grounding me when everything else feels like it's spinning out of control.

"Define ready," Gray mutters, but he nods.

Bree takes a deep breath, squaring her shoulders in a way that reminds me why I fell for her in the first place. She's scared — terrified, really — but she's not backing down.

"Let's go find out what's waiting for us," she says.

And despite everything — the fear, the uncertainty, the very real possibility that we're walking into something that could destroy us all — I find myself grinning.

"That's my girl."

The walk through the sanctuary grounds starts out deceptively normal.

Once we clear the small homes that Bree and her Ether created, we're greeted by birds chirping in the trees. Sunlight filtering through the canopy in those picture-perfect shafts that make everything look like a fairy tale. The kind of peaceful morning that makes you forget there are ancient horrors lurking just beneath the surface of the world.

"Anyone else feel like we're walking into the opening scene of a horror movie?" I ask, stepping over a fallen log. "You know, the part where the overly confident comic relief makes a joke right before everything goes to shit?"

"Jace," Rhett warns, but there's no real heat in it.

"What? I'm just saying, if I suddenly start monologuing about how nothing could possibly go wrong, someone should probably tackle me."

Bree actually cracks a smile at that, and I count it as a victory. She's been quiet since we left, walking between Gray and Wes like she needs the buffer.

Her Ether curls around her ankles in restless silver threads, occasionally sparking with those dark veins that make my skin crawl.

"How much further?" she asks Theo, who's been leading us with the single-minded determination of someone following a GPS that only exists in his head.

"Not far," he says, but his voice is tight. "I can feel it. Like a... pull."

"That's comforting," Stellan murmurs from behind us.

We've been walking for maybe twenty minutes when the forest starts to change. Nothing dramatic at first — just a gradual shift in the quality of light, the way sound seems to muffle and echo at the same time. The trees grow closer together, their branches intertwining overhead until the canopy blocks out most of the sky.

"Is it just me," Wes says quietly, "or does it feel like the trees are watching us?"

I glance around and have to suppress a shiver. He's not wrong. There's something about the way the shadows fall, the way the leaves seem to rustle without any wind, that sets my teeth on edge.

"It's the Ether," Bree says, her voice barely above a whisper. "It's... responding to something. I can feel it."

As if on cue, her Ether flares brighter, silver light dancing between the trees like foxfire. The black threads pulse through it, and I watch Thane's expression tighten.

"Maybe we should—" Gray starts, but Theo suddenly stops dead in his tracks.

"There," he breathes.

I follow his gaze and feel my smart-ass grin die on my lips.

At first glance, it looks like nothing much — just a clearing in the trees with some old stones scattered around. Nothing that would catch your attention unless you knew to look for it.

But as we get closer, I can see what made Theo's breath catch. Carved into every visible stone surface are symbols — spirals and curves that hurt to look at directly, like they're moving just outside the edge of vision. And scattered among the ancient stones, catching light that shouldn't exist in the shadow of the trees, are pieces of broken mirror.

"Well," I say, my voice coming out rougher than I intended. "That's weird."

Bree takes a step forward, and her Ether surges like a tide. The symbols begin to pulse with faint light, and the mirror shards start to gleam like they're reflecting something that isn't there.

"Bree," Rhett says, a warning in his voice.

But she's not listening. She's staring at the ruins like she's seeing a ghost, her face pale but determined.

"It's real," she whispers. "Theo, you were right. It's all real."

The air around us thickens, charged with the kind of electric potential that makes your hair stand on end. And then the ground beneath the scattered stones starts to shift.

Not violently — more like breathing. Like the earth itself is exhaling after holding its breath for centuries.

The center of the clearing sinks inward, revealing what was hidden beneath. Stone steps, worn smooth by age, spiraling down into darkness so complete it seems to swallow light.

Whatever's down there, whatever's been waiting in the dark — it knows we're here.

And it knows she's here.

I look at the faces around me — fear, determination, resignation. We all know we're about to cross a line we can't uncross. Walk into something that's going to change everything.

"So," I say, keeping my voice light because someone has to. "Anyone want to bet those pancakes I promised are going to be the 'holy-shit-we-survived' variety?"

Bree looks back at me, and for just a moment, I see a flicker of the young girl who used to laugh at my jokes. Before Ethos. Before the Crown. Before everything got so fucking complicated.

"Only one way to find out," she says, placing her foot on the top step.

What the fuck have we gotten ourselves into?

Chapter 32
BREE

I stand at the edge of the opening, staring down into darkness that seems to pull at something deep in my chest. The stone steps spiral down beyond what I can see, worn smooth by ages of footsteps that came before. Before me. Before this moment that feels like it's been waiting my whole life.

The Ether coils around my ankles, restless silver threads shot through with black that pulse in rhythm with my heartbeat. It wants to go down. I can feel it tugging at me like a tide, like gravity, like coming home.

"Bree." Rhett's voice carries a warning I've heard too many times lately. "Maybe we should—"

"No." The word comes out sharper than I intend, but I don't take it back. "This is mine. Whatever's down there, it's mine."

I can feel them all watching me — Rhett's protective tension, Gray's quiet concern, Jace's restless energy. Wes hovers close enough that I can sense his warmth, and Theo stands perfectly still like he's afraid any movement might shatter the moment.

Thane and Stellan are silent, standing apart from the others, though something in their stillness feels different. Expectant. Like they know exactly what I'm about to find.

"I'll go first," I say, not looking back at them. "Alone."

"Like hell," Jace starts, but I cut him off.

"This isn't a discussion." My voice carries an authority I didn't know I had in me, and it surprises me as much as it does them. "I can feel it calling to me. Not to us. To me."

The Ether flares brighter, and the symbols carved into the scattered stones begin to pulse in response. The mirror shards catch the light and throw it back in patterns that would look beautiful if there weren't angry butterflies in my stomach.

I take the first step down.

The moment my foot touches the ancient stone, the world changes.

Light blooms along the walls — not harsh, but warm and welcoming, like coming inside from the cold. The darkness retreats, revealing carved symbols that spiral down the walls in patterns that seem to move when I'm not looking directly at them.

Each step I take, more light appears. Not electric or fire, but something else. Something that recognizes me.

"Bree?" Gray's voice echoes from above, careful and concerned.

"I'm okay," I call back, though my voice sounds strange in this space. Richer somehow. Like the walls are designed to carry sound.

The stairs curve as they descend, and with each turn, I can see more of what waits below. My breath catches.

It's not just a room. It's a cathedral.

The staircase opens into a circular chamber so vast I can't see the far walls in the gentle light that emanates from the stones themselves. The air is cooler here, carrying the faint scent of old stone and something that might be ozone, like the aftermath of lightning.

But what steals my breath isn't the size — it's the design.

The chamber descends in tiers around me, like an ancient amphitheater built in reverse. Stone platforms extend down in concentric circles, each level carved with alcoves and niches, creating rings that spiral so far down toward shadows that light can't penetrate. And mounted on every wall, are mirrors.

Hundreds of them.

Each one is different — some tall and narrow, others wide and ornate, all of them framed in materials I don't recognize but that seem to shimmer with their own inner light. They line every tier, creating a constellation of reflecting surfaces that catches and multiplies the ambient glow.

I reach the bottom of the stairs and step onto the smooth floor.

The chamber responds.

Light races along the carved symbols, following pathways etched into the stone that connect every mirror to every other mirror in an intricate web of silver lines. The mirrors themselves begin to glow softly around their edges, not reflecting my image but something deeper. Something waiting.

"Oh," I breathe.

I take a step toward the nearest ring of mirrors, and the Ether around me surges like a breaking wave.

The first mirror I approach shows my reflection — but different. The girl looking back at me has the same face, the same dark hair, the same green eyes. But she stands straighter. Looks more certain. There's no fear in her expression, no hesitation.

She looks like someone who knows exactly who she is.

"Riley," I whisper, and the name echoes in the chamber like recognition.

The mirror ripples at the sound, and I swear she moves independently. Her head tilts as she meets my eyes directly. My reflection isn't mine anymore.

"Finally," she says, her voice carrying across the chamber like she's standing right next to me instead of trapped behind glass. "I was beginning to think you'd never find me."

My knees nearly buckle. "You're real. This is real."

"As real as you are." She speaks, pressing hand against the inside of the mirror. "Though I suppose that's relative, isn't it? You're there, I'm here, and between us is... well. Everything."

"I don't understand." The words tumble out. "What is this place? What happened here? What am I supposed to do?"

Riley's expression softens with something that might be sympathy. "You really don't know, do you? They kept you in the dark about everything."

Above us, I can hear footsteps on the stairs. Careful, cautious, but coming nonetheless. Part of me wants to call out, tell them to stay back, that this moment feels too fragile for witnesses.

But another part — a larger part — knows that whatever happens next, I want them here. I want them to see.

"They're important to you," Riley says, and there's something wistful in her voice. "I can feel them."

"They are." The words come out easier than I expect. "They matter."

"Even the ones who scare you? Even the ones you're not sure you can trust?"

Images flash through my mind — Thane's silver eyes going soft when he thinks no one is looking, Stellan's careful distance that somehow feels like protection, the way Wes looks at me like I'm something precious and breakable and worth saving.

"Especially them," I say quietly.

Riley smiles. "Good. That matters more than you know."

Behind me, I hear Rhett's voice: "Bree? Everything okay down there?"

"Come down," I call back, not taking my eyes off Riley. "All of you. I think... I think you need to see this too."

The sound of multiple footsteps echoes down the stairs, and I can feel the exact moment when each of them sees the chamber. Jace goes silent. Gray mutters a curse. Wes's soft "Holy shit."

And from Thane, though I can barely hear him: "The mirrors are intact."

Stellan says, even quieter: "But look at the floor."

I follow his gaze and see them — small piles of ash scattered across the chamber floor, each one positioned in front of a mirror. Some mirrors have no ash at all, others have multiple piles, like someone arranged them deliberately.

The ash looks like it's been sitting here untouched for centuries.

"What is that?" I ask, but no one answers.

"Bree." Thane's voice cuts through the moment, sharp with something that might be fear. "Step back from the mirrors."

"Now," Stellan adds, and there's an edge to his usual composure that makes my skin prickle. "Whatever you're feeling, whatever's calling to you — resist it."

I look between them, startled by the urgency in their voices. "What? Why? What's wrong?"

They spread out around the outer edge of the chamber, but instead of the awed silence I expected, there's tension crackling between them. Rhett's hands are clenched, ready for a fight while Gray looks like he wants to physically drag me away from the mirrors.

But it's the look on Thane and Stellan's faces that really gets to me. I've never seen either of them scared before. And they are definitely scared right now.

"What aren't you telling me?" I ask.

Thane and Stellan exchange a look, and I see something pass between them. A decision.

"This place has a history," Stellan says carefully. "People have tried... the Oath. It didn't end well."

"Those ash piles," Thane adds, his voice tight, "are from people who tried... and failed."

"What?" The word comes out sharp. "What oath? What are you talking about?"

"People who tried to use the mirrors without understanding what they were doing," Stellan says. "Without having what was needed."

"The chamber responded to you," Gray says quietly from behind me. "The lights, the symbols — none of that happened when Theo and Seth found this place."

"You brought them," Riley says, approval clear in her voice. "Good."

But I can feel the fear still radiating from Thane and Stellan now, the way they're watching every movement of my Ether with barely contained panic.

Riley's voice carries across the chamber again, softer now. "This is the first time in centuries this chamber has come awake. The first time the mirrors have responded to anyone."

I turn back to look at Riley. "What does that mean?"

"It means you have what they didn't," she says simply. "What they were all missing."

Riley studies me for a long moment, then glances at the others behind me. "Not here. Not yet. There are things you need to know first. Questions that need answers."

"But you're here. Can't you just tell me?"

"Some knowledge has to come from the living world." Riley's smile turns gentle. "From people who chose to trust you with the truth. But I can tell you this much — when the time comes, the choice will be yours alone. And whatever you choose will be right."

"What choice? What are you talking about?"

Riley's expression grows sad. "Ask them. They know more than they've told you." Her eyes flick to Thane and Stellan. "Don't they?"

The mirror begins to dim slightly, and I feel a flutter of panic.

"Don't go," I say quickly. "I just found you."

"I'm not going anywhere." Riley presses her hand to the glass again. "I'll be here when you're ready. When you understand what you're choosing."

The light in the mirror fades until it shows only my own reflection again. But something has changed. The girl looking back at me isn't perfect or certain or unafraid. But she's not broken either. She's just... me. Real and flawed and that's okay.

I turn back to face the guys, still shaken by everything that just happened. Riley's words echo in my head, and I can feel the weight of all the questions I don't have answers to.

I look at Thane, then Stellan. "We need to talk." My eyes sweep over the rest of them. "All of us."

"So," Jace says, voice rough with emotion he's trying to hide behind humor. "How about those we-made-it-out-alive pancakes? We've earned it."

I shoot him a look.

"Fine. Pancakes and explanations. Now."

Chapter 33
WES

I can't sit still.

We just got back from the chamber maybe twenty minutes ago, and my skin feels like it's been stretched too tight across my bones. The trek back was silent—all of us lost in our own heads, trying to process what we'd witnessed. Bree went straight to the kitchen the moment we walked through the sanctuary doors, and the rest of us are wandering around like we don't know how to be around each other anymore.

The hunger won't let me settle.

Not the usual gnawing emptiness I've gotten used to. This is sharper, more focused. It started shifting that night—Bree giving without flinching, like there was nothing wrong with needing. And then Gray, steady and stubborn, holding me there like I wasn't going to break him. Different, but both of them hit something I didn't know I was starving for. Since then the hunger doesn't just sit in me—it watches, listens. Feels every crack in the room. The tight line of Gray's jaw. The way Jace keeps flexing his hands like he's ready to throw something.

How Bree's absence feels like a missing piece of myself.

I pad down the hallway toward the kitchen, bare feet silent on cool stone. Pancakes and explanations, Bree said. So here we are, heading toward the conversation none of us want to have but can't avoid.

The scent hits me before I reach the doorway—vanilla, butter, something warm and sweet that makes my mouth water.

I round the corner and stop.

Jace is at the stove, still in the clothes we wore to the chamber, hair disheveled from the trek back, but his hands move with the practiced confidence of someone who's done this a thousand times. A stack of golden pancakes sits on a plate beside him—perfectly round, fluffy, the kind he's been perfecting since we all met.

He flips a pancake with the theatrical flair I've come to expect, shoulders relaxing slightly when he sees me. "Right on time for the grand unveiling." He gestures at his work with mock ceremony. "Behold—Sanctuary Supremes. Patent pending."

Despite everything, I almost smile. "Sanctuary Supremes?"

"Golden perfection. Fluffy clouds of breakfast joy. The antidote to cosmic horror." He finally glances at me, and there's something different in his expression. More settled, maybe. Less like he's performing and more like he's just... here. "Want one?"

"Yeah." I settle onto one of the stools, watching him work. There's something soothing about the ritual of it—the precise pour of batter, the patient wait for bubbles to form, the satisfying flip. Normal. Human. Safe.

"So," Jace says, not looking at me. "That was a thing that happened."

I snort. "Understatement of the century."

"Want to talk about it?"

I consider that. The chamber. The mirrors. The way Bree looked when she spoke Riley's name—like she was seeing something the rest of us couldn't. The ash under our feet and the feeling that we were standing in a place that remembered choices that had gone wrong.

"I don't know if I can," I admit. "It felt like... like we weren't supposed to be there. But also like we had to be."

Jace nods slowly. "Yeah. Like the place was waiting for her specifically, but it wanted witnesses."

"The way it responded to her..." I shake my head. "That wasn't just magic. That was recognition."

"Recognition of what?"

Before I can answer, the sound of footsteps echoes from the hallway. Jace immediately goes rigid, hand tightening on the spatula.

"Don't touch my pancakes," he says without turning around. "I'm serious, Wes. These are art."

I look over my shoulder. "It's not me you need to worry about."

Gray appears in the doorway, hair damp like he just got out of the shower. He takes in the scene—Jace at the stove, the stack of pancakes, my position at the counter—and something shifts in his expression. Not quite a smile, but close.

"Pancakes and explanations," he says, echoing Bree's words from earlier.

"That was the deal," I confirm.

He moves closer, and I catch the scent of soap and something uniquely him. My awareness sharpens, that new hunger stirring to life. It's not uncomfortable exactly, but it's... noticeable. The way he moves, the quiet strength in his presence, the way he glances at Jace with something soft in his eyes.

"Need to use the bathroom," Jace announces suddenly, setting down the spatula carefully because he's someone who takes his cooking seriously. "These are at a critical stage. Do. Not. Touch. Anything."

He points at both of us with mock severity, then disappears down the hallway.

Gray and I look at each other. Then at the pancakes.

"He's very serious about his breakfast today," Gray observes.

"Apparently they're Sanctuary Supremes."

"Patent pending?"

"Patent pending."

We share a look that's almost normal. Almost like we're not all reeling from whatever happened in that chamber. Almost like my skin isn't humming with awareness of how close he's standing.

That's when Mairen bustles in.

"Oh!" She stops short, taking in the scene with bright eyes. "I'm so sorry, darlings—I missed breakfast prep, didn't I?" She surveys Jace's setup with the efficiency of someone who's spent decades in kitchens. "Well, no matter. I'll just get a batch going—"

"Actually," I start, but she's already moving.

And by moving, I mean completely taking over.

She ties on an apron that wasn't there a moment ago, examines Jace's batter with a critical eye, then begins... improving. A splash of vanilla that wasn't in the original recipe. A pinch of something that smells like cinnamon but warmer. She adjusts the heat on the stove, tests the pan with a drop of water that sizzles and dances.

"Um," Gray says. "Jace is pretty particular about—"

"Oh, these will be lovely," Mairen says cheerfully, pouring perfect circles of batter that somehow look more golden than Jace's. "Much fluffier than mine usually turn out."

I watch in fascination as she works. There's something almost magical about it—the way she moves like she's been using this kitchen for years, how the pancakes seem to cook faster and more evenly under her attention. Even the smell is better, richer somehow.

The laughter when Gray and I exchange looks tastes warm and golden, but it doesn't touch the deeper hunger. Nothing really does except—

"Mairen," I say carefully, pushing the thought away. "Jace has a very specific process—"

"Does he? How lovely." She flips three pancakes simultaneously without looking. All perfect. "Young men should have passions."

Gray catches my eye over her head, and I can see he's trying not to laugh.

That's when Jace returns.

He rounds the corner talking. "—probably overthinking it, but the chamber felt like it was testing us somehow, like it wanted to see if we'd—"

He stops. Stares.

His carefully organized station has been completely reorganized. The batter bowl is in a different spot. There are new ingredients on the counter he definitely didn't put there. Mairen is at his stove, humming softly, making pancakes with his recipe but somehow better.

The look on his face is pure betrayal.

"What," he says slowly, "is happening to my Sanctuary Supremes?"

Mairen looks up with a brilliant smile. "Oh, you're back! I was just helping—"

"Helping?" Jace's voice climbs an octave. "Those are not Sanctuary Supremes. You can't just—there's a process, Mairen! A specific technique!"

"Is there? How wonderful." She plates another stack of golden perfection. "These are turning out beautifully."

I watch Jace's face cycle through several emotions. Outrage. Disbelief. A growing horror as he realizes that her version actually does smell better.

"You moved my vanilla," he says weakly.

"Just a touch more. Brings out the flavor."

"And you changed the temperature."

"Medium-low works better for even cooking."

"Those aren't my pancakes anymore."

Mairen pats his arm gently. "They're better pancakes, dear."

Jace looks at Gray and me like we're his last hope for justice in an unjust world. "Tell her. Tell her about pancake jurisdiction. About sacred breakfast territory."

Gray's lips are twitching. "Well—"

"This is a violation," Jace continues dramatically. "A culinary coup. An overthrow of established pancake government."

That's when Rhett and Theo appear, ready to get this Oath conversation over with.

"Explanation time?" Rhett asks, taking in the scene.

"Mairen made better pancakes," I explain.

"They're not better," Jace protests. "They're different. Illegally different."

Theo picks up one of Mairen's pancakes and takes a bite. His eyebrows rise. "These are really good."

"Traitor," Jace mutters.

"Try one," Mairen offers, holding out the plate to Jace with maternal patience.

He eyes it like it might bite him. "I already know what my pancakes taste like."

"These aren't your pancakes, remember?" Gray points out. "These are illegal pancakes."

"Exactly—" Jace stops, glares at him. "You're not helping."

"Just try it," I say.

Jace takes the pancake like he's accepting evidence of his own failure. Bites it. Chews slowly.

His expression goes through another cycle. This time ending on grudging admiration.

"Fine," he mutters. "They're good."

"They're better than good," Theo says around another bite.

"They're not Sanctuary Supremes though," Jace insists. "They're... they're..."

"Superior Sanctuary Stacks?" I suggest.

Jace points at all of us accusingly. "You're all banned from my kitchen."

"Is it still your kitchen if Mairen's the one making the food?" Theo asks innocently.

Before Jace can respond to that devastating blow, footsteps echo from the main hallway. Heavier. More deliberate.

Stellan appears in the doorway.

He takes in the scene with that particular stillness of his—Mairen at the stove, Jace's theatrical outrage, the rest of us gathered around like we're watching dinner theater. His gray eyes scan the group, noting who's here and who's not.

"Domestic bliss," he observes. "How charming."

There's something in his tone that makes the easy humor drain out of the room. Not cruel, exactly but like he's seeing something the rest of us are missing.

"Explanations," Rhett explains when Stellan's gray eyes scan the group. "That was the deal."

"I can see that." Stellan moves further into the kitchen, his presence immediately shifting the energy. "Though I suspect the truth won't be as comforting as Jace's... or Mairen's cooking."

The chamber. Riley. The ash and mirrors and the feeling that we'd stepped into a place that shouldn't exist.

The lightness evaporates completely.

"What was that place?" Gray asks quietly.

"Ancient," a soft voice says from the window. "Sacred. And... waiting."

We all turn. Everyone—Stellan, Thane, Rhett, Theo, even Mairen—looks surprised to see Bree standing there. Like we'd all somehow forgotten she was in the room.

She turns from the window to face us, and there's something different in her expression. Older, maybe. More certain. Like the girl who spoke Riley's name and meant it. The mist that usually curls around her seems darker too—silver shot through with larger threads of black. It moves differently, more restless, than I've seen before.

"You've all been talking around me," she continues, her voice steady despite the way her hands shake slightly. "But I was there. I saw her. I know what that chamber is, even if I don't understand it yet."

The silence stretches, heavy with the weight of everything unsaid.

Stellan doesn't answer immediately. He accepts a mug of coffee from Mairen with a nod of thanks, then leans against the counter in a way that makes every gesture look deliberate.

"She's not wrong," he says finally, his gray eyes fixing on Bree with something that might be approval. "Though 'waiting' is perhaps understating it."

"That's not really an answer," Jace points out.

"Isn't it?" Stellan's mouth quirks. "Your pancakes are rituals, Jace. The chamber we found is just older. And more patient."

Something cold settles in my stomach. "More patient how?"

"It wants something," Stellan says simply. "Something it's been waiting centuries to claim."

"Bree," Theo says. It's not a question.

Stellan inclines his head. "The last of her line. The only one left who can give it what it needs."

"Which is what?" Rhett demands.

But before Stellan can answer, another voice cuts through the kitchen.

"Completion."

We all turn. Thane stands in the doorway, silver eyes unreadable and his usual composure frayed at the edges.

"The chamber is bound to an ancient rite," he continues, moving into the room with that predatory grace of his. "One that was forbidden for good reason."

Stellan's expression sharpens with something that might be approval. Or warning.

"The Ashen Oath," Thane says, and the words seem to hang in the air like a death sentence.

None of us speak. The name makes something cold coil in my stomach. Like hearing it changes something fundamental, makes whatever happened in that chamber more real.

"What's the Ashen Oath?" I ask, though part of me doesn't want to know.

Stellan and Thane exchange a look—brief, loaded with something the rest of us don't get.

"Sit down," Stellan says finally. "This will take a while."

We arrange ourselves around the kitchen island, pancakes forgotten. Mairen continues cooking like she's not listening, but I notice how still she's gone. How her movements have become more careful, more quiet.

Even she knows we're about to learn something that changes everything.

Stellan sets down his mug, and when he speaks, his voice carries the weight of centuries.

"The Ashen Oath is the last rite of the Ether Source line," he begins. "A binding between the self and its reflection. Between what is and what could be."

My chest tightens. The chamber. The mirrors. The ash under our feet.

"It requires a choice," Thane adds, his silver eyes fixed on some point beyond us. "One that can't be undone. The Council has kept it buried for good reason."

Stellan and Thane exchange another look—brief, loaded with something the rest of us don't get. There's something in that silence, something they're not saying.

The hunger in me sharpens, clawing toward something I don't understand. Toward Bree and what she's being pulled toward.

And toward the growing certainty that whatever Stellan tells us next will change everything.

233

Chapter 34
STELLAN

Children playing at gods, sitting in a kitchen eating pancakes, about to hear the oldest story they'll ever know.

I watch them arrange themselves around the island—Jace still sulking about his culinary territory being invaded, Rhett radiating heat even while somewhat calm, Wes restless with that hunger threading through him I know too well. Gray sits with his usual careful stillness, but I can see the tension in the line of his shoulders. Theo's already gone quiet, his eyes distant like he's seeing fragments of what I'm about to tell them.

Even Mairen has stilled completely, her hands motionless on the counter. She knows. Perhaps not the specifics, but she recognizes the weight of what's about to be spoken.

The Ashen Oath. A name I haven't said aloud in decades, though it's lived in my thoughts like a sleeping serpent ever since I laid eyes on her. Beautiful in ways that unsettle me, everything I didn't know I was starving for wrapped in scars and uncertainty. The pull toward her defies every rule I've built around myself, every careful distance I maintain. And that terrifies me more than the Oath itself.

"The last rite of the Source line," I begin, keeping my voice level, controlled. "A binding between what you are and what waits in the mirror."

I pause, letting that settle. Watch their faces process the implications.

"Most believe it never worked," I continue, allowing a thread of doubt to color my words. "Centuries of ash don't lie. But then again—" I glance at Thane, and he catches my meaning immediately. "Centuries of suppression might explain the failures better than flawed ritual."

Thane leans forward, silver eyes sharp. "If it never worked, why was it banned? Why does the Council still fear it?" His voice takes on that cutting political edge. "They're not protecting us from myth, Stellan. They're protecting their power."

There it is. The seed planted. Let them think this is about Council politics, about power structures they can understand. They're not ready for the deeper truth—that some of us have been waiting centuries for exactly this moment.

"What does it actually do?" Gray asks, cutting straight to the heart of it. Always practical, our Gray.

"Two paths," I explain, settling into the rhythm of revelation. "The first—complete fusion. Two halves becoming whole. The power would be..." I pause, searching for words that won't terrify them completely. "Exponential. Unlike anything the magical world has seen since the Source lines ruled."

Wes shifts in his seat, and I can taste the hunger coming off him—sharp, curious, afraid. Good. He should be afraid.

"And the second?" Theo asks quietly.

"Remaining separate but Oath-bound. Resonance between the selves, shared strength across the Human Realm and the Mirror Realm, but maintaining individual identity." I keep my tone neutral, though I know which path calls to me more strongly. "Less power, but more... sustainable."

"The chamber recognizes bloodline," Thane adds, his voice taking on that formal Council tone. "It woke for her because she's the first. The one who must open the path. Once she takes the Oath, once the Ether Source magic flows through the ritual again..." He pauses, the implications hanging heavy. "The door opens for everyone else."

"So I'm the key." Bree's voice cuts through the silence, steady and clear. She's leaning against the window still, but there's something different in her posture now. Less uncertain, more... present. "Not just for myself, but for everyone."

The mist around her shifts, and I notice the black threads seem less chaotic now, more deliberate. Like they're responding to her growing understanding rather than overwhelming her.

Rhett's hands clench on the counter. "And you're telling us this because...?"

"Because the chamber is awake now." I pause, watching their faces. "It knows she exists. It will call to her. The pull will only get stronger until she answers."

"Good." Bree pushes away from the window, moving closer to the group. There's something almost regal in the way she carries herself now, like she's finally stepping into a space that was always meant for her. "I'm tired of things happening to me. Of being pulled and pushed and told what I am without understanding why."

The Ether moves with her, and I can feel the power radiating off her—not wild or reactive like before, but controlled. Purposeful.

What I don't say: I want to be there when she does. I want to witness the moment she chooses—not just between paths, but between versions of herself. There's something intoxicating about that level of transformation, that absolute commitment to becoming.

"Can someone force her?" Jace asks, his usual humor absent. "Make the choice for her?"

"No." The word comes out sharp. I modulate my tone, make it reassuring. "The Oath recognizes only willing consent. Coercion would cause the chamber to reject the attempt entirely."

True, as far as it goes. What I don't mention is that willing consent can be... cultivated. Encouraged. That hunger and fear and need can make choices feel inevitable when they're really just seductive.

"But she doesn't understand any of this," Wes says, and there's something raw in his voice. "She doesn't know what she's walking into."

"No," I agree. "She doesn't."

And that innocence is part of what makes her so compelling. Bree approaches her power like someone discovering fire—awed, afraid, but unable to resist reaching toward the flame. When she finally understands the true scope of what the Oath offers, when she feels the pull of becoming something larger than herself...

I find myself curious which path she'll choose. Fusion would make her magnificent—terrible and complete, a force that could reshape the magical world. But separation would leave room for bonds, for connection, for the kind of intimacy that feeds something deeper than simple hunger.

Both possibilities fascinate me in different ways.

"What happens to the chamber if she refuses?" Gray asks. "If she just... walks away?"

Thane and I exchange a look. This is the question I hoped they wouldn't ask.

"The chamber has been awakened," I say carefully. "It has tasted Ether, recognized bloodline. Walking away isn't really an option anymore."

The silence that follows carries the weight of understanding. Not just that Bree faces a choice, but that the choice is inevitable. The Oath will have her answer, one way or another.

Mairen finally moves, setting down a plate of perfectly golden pancakes with deliberate gentleness. The domestic gesture feels surreal against the backdrop of ancient magic and impossible choices. Golden pancakes cooling between us, and yet the taste in the air is ash.

"You'll need to decide soon," Thane says quietly as he locks eyes with Bree. "The longer the chamber waits, the more unstable it becomes. And there are... other parties who might take interest in what's been awakened. Not all of them want this power returned to the world."

I keep my expression neutral, but inside, something sharp and hungry unfurls. "Correct," I say simply. "Others will come. There are those who would kill for the chance at the Oath, and others who would kill to keep it buried. Some prefer their myths to stay mythical, even when they know the truth."

And if the rumors I've been tracking are true, if there really is something moving in the spaces between realms...

The thought of Bree caught between competing hungers, forced to choose not just paths but protectors, sends heat through my veins.

"We protect her," Rhett says, and it's not a question.

"You protect each other," Bree corrects, and there's something almost commanding in her tone. "I won't hide behind anyone anymore. If I'm going to do this—" She pauses, the mist around her pulsing once like a heartbeat. "When I do this, I do it as myself. All of myself."

"Of course," I agree smoothly. "But protection and guidance aren't the same thing. You'll need to understand your options fully before you choose."

What I don't say: I intend to be part of that understanding. To help her see not just the risks, but the rewards. The exquisite possibility of becoming something more than human fear and mortal limitation.

The chamber has been waiting for centuries.

And now, so am I—watching, patient, hungry for the moment she finally chooses.

Chapter 35
RHETT

I'm nervous.

I raise my hand to knock, then drop it and pace to the other end of the hallway. "This is stupid," I mutter under my breath. The sanctuary is quiet, everyone else finally asleep after today's revelations about the Ashen Oath, about Riley, about the choice that's coming whether we're ready or not.

But that's not why I'm here, standing outside her door like some lovesick teenager.

"What the hell is your problem?" I shake my head, stepping back in front of her door. It's just Bree. Bree, who I've known for years. Bree, who I've been keeping careful distance from because I'm terrified of making things worse.

I take a breath and raise my hand again to knock.

Then drop it again.

Christ. This is pathetic.

The distance has been eating me alive. The careful space she's been keeping between us since Phil, since everything went to hell. I get it—I do. But watching her today, seeing the look in her eyes when Stellan explained what the chamber wants from her... Not afraid, exactly. Resigned. Like she's already accepted that she'll face it alone.

That's what breaks me.

I raise my fist and knock before I can chicken out again. Soft, but firm enough that she'll hear.

"Bree?" I keep my voice low. "It's me."

Silence stretches long enough that I wonder if she's ignoring me. Then footsteps, quiet on the stone floor, and the door opens.

She's wearing an oversized t-shirt that hangs to her thighs, hair mussed like she was trying to sleep. But her eyes are too bright, too alert. She hasn't been sleeping any better than I have.

"Rhett." Her voice is careful, neutral. "Everything okay?"

"No," I say simply. "Can I come in?"

She hesitates, and that small pause cuts deeper than it should. But then she steps back, holding the door open.

Her room is exactly what I expected—warm colors, soft textures, the sanctuary's way of responding to her needs. Small changes since we first arrived, but it feels different tonight. Smaller somehow, like the space between us is taking up too much room.

She settles on the edge of her bed, tucking her legs under herself. I stay near the door, suddenly uncertain.

"Bree, I—" I stop, run a hand through my hair. "I'm sorry."

"For what?"

"For pulling back. For keeping my distance when you needed me to stay close." The words taste like ash, but they're true. "For letting my fear make your trauma worse."

Her green eyes search my face. "Rhett—"

"I was so scared of hurting you that I ended up doing exactly that." My hands clench at my sides, heat flickering under my skin. "When

Phil—when I realized I should have been there, should have protected you—"

"You couldn't have known."

"But I should have stayed closer." The admission tears out of me. "I should have trusted that you'd tell me if I was too much, instead of deciding for you. Instead of making you feel like you had to handle everything alone."

She's quiet for a long moment, studying me with those too-perceptive eyes. "I don't forgive you yet," she says finally, and the honesty is brutal. "I'm still angry. Still hurt."

My chest tightens, but I nod. "I know."

"But I miss you." Her voice goes softer. "I miss us. How we used to be."

"I miss you too." The words come out rougher than I intended. "God, Bree, I miss you so much it's like missing a limb."

Something shifts in her expression—surprise, maybe, at the raw honesty. But she deserves it. She unfolds herself from the bed, moves closer. Not touching, but close enough. I close my eyes, taking in her scent. I can smell her shampoo, and everything else that makes her smell like her. Like my Bree.

When I open my eyes, she's watching me with something that looks like decision.

"I want you," she says simply.

The mist around her feet stirs at her words, responding not just to arousal but to the raw honesty in her voice. Silver threads pulse once, like her Ether recognizes truth when she speaks it.

The honesty of it, the permission wrapped in truth, undoes something in my chest. "Are you sure?"

Instead of answering, she closes the distance between us, rises on her toes, and kisses me.

It's different from before—not desperate or uncertain, but deliberate. She kisses me like she's choosing me, even with all the fractures between us. Like want can exist alongside hurt, like desire doesn't require forgiveness.

When she pulls back, her cheeks are flushed, her breathing uneven. "Show me," she says.

"Show you what?"

"How much you missed me."

The words break what's left of my control. I cup her face in my hands, kiss her like I'm trying to pour weeks of regret and longing into the connection. She responds immediately, her hands fisting in my shirt, pulling me closer until there's no space left between us.

The kiss deepens quickly, relief and apology tangled in the desperate press of our mouths. My hands are tentative at first, skimming over her waist, her back, like I'm afraid she'll change her mind. But when she pulls me closer, when she makes that soft sound against my lips, something in me snaps.

My hands grip her tighter, one sliding up to tangle in her hair, the other pressing against the small of her back. She tastes like mint and something uniquely her, and I can't get enough.

"Off," she breathes against my mouth, tugging at my shirt.

My hands shake as I pull it over my head, and she's already reaching for the hem of hers. When she lifts it away, revealing the soft curves of her breasts, I forget how to breathe.

"God, Bree," I whisper, my voice rough. "You're so beautiful."

Her cheeks flush, but she doesn't look away. Instead, she reaches for my belt, fingers fumbling with the buckle in her urgency.

"Let me," I say, but my own hands are trembling so badly I can't get the damn thing undone.

She laughs—actually laughs—and pushes my hands away. "Here, let me before you break it."

"Smooth, firefighter," I mutter to myself, heat creeping up my neck.

"Don't worry." She gets my belt undone with efficient fingers, then looks up at me with soft eyes. "I'm nervous too."

"You are?"

"Of course I am." She tugs my jeans down my hips. "This matters, Rhett. You matter."

She helps me out of my jeans when I hesitate, and then we're both naked, skin against skin for the first time. The sensation is overwhelming—her warmth, the softness of her body pressed against mine.

I lift her easily, her legs wrapping around my waist as I carry her to the bed. When I lay her down, she's looking at me with something that takes my breath away—want and tenderness and trust all tangled together.

I start at her mouth, kissing her deeply before trailing down her throat. When I reach her breasts, I take my time, learning the weight of them in my hands, the way her nipples peak under my tongue.

"Rhett," she gasps when I suck gently, her back arching off the bed.

The sound of my name like that nearly undoes me. I worship each breast with reverent attention, my hands moving down, mapping the curve of her waist, the flare of her hips. Her skin is so soft, so warm under my palms.

When I kiss my way down her stomach, she goes very still.

"You don't have to—" she starts.

"I want to taste you," I say, looking up at her. "Please."

Her breath hitches. "Okay."

I settle between her thighs, and the sight of her—pink and glistening and ready—makes my mouth water. The first tentative lick makes her hips buck, a broken moan escaping her throat.

She tastes incredible—salt and sweetness and something that's purely her. I'm clumsy at first, trying to figure out what she likes, but I follow her responses. When I find her clit with my tongue, she cries out.

"There," she gasps, one hand threading through my hair. "Oh God, right there."

I focus on that spot, alternating between gentle licks and firmer pressure. Her thighs start to shake around my head, and I slide two fingers inside her, feeling how wet and tight she is.

"Fuck," she breathes, her hips moving against my mouth. "Don't stop."

I work her with my tongue and fingers until she's trembling, until she's making sounds I want to memorize forever. But when I try to add a third finger, I'm clumsy, and she winces.

"Shit, sorry—"

"It's okay," she breathes, but I pull back anyway.

"I'm sorry. I'm still figuring this out."

"Hey." She sits up on her elbows, looking at me with those green eyes. "You're doing fine. Better than fine. Just—" She reaches down, covering my hand with hers, guiding my fingers. "Like this. Feel that?"

I follow her guidance, and when she moans, the sound goes straight through me.

"Yeah," I say roughly. "I feel it."

"Good. Now—oh God, yes—just like that."

But before she can come, she's pulling at my shoulders.

"I need you inside me," she says, voice strained with want. "Please, Rhett. Now."

I kiss my way back up her body, settling between her thighs. My cock is hard and aching, pressing against her entrance. But suddenly, the weight of the moment hits me.

"I need to tell you something," I say, my voice rough.

Her eyes search my face. "What?"

"I've never—" I swallow hard. "With anyone. I was waiting. For you."

Her pupils dilate, surprise and arousal mixing in her expression. "You're a virgin?"

"Yeah." Heat creeps up my neck. "I know it's—"

She cuts me off with a kiss, deep and possessive. "That's so fucking hot," she whispers against my mouth.

The words send fire straight through me. She reaches between us, wrapping her hand around my cock, and I nearly lose it at the contact.

"I want to be your first," she says, guiding me to her entrance.

When I start to push inside, the sensation is overwhelming. She's so tight, so wet, so incredibly hot around me. I have to grit my teeth and go slow, watching her face for any sign of discomfort.

"Fuck," I breathe, stopping halfway. "You feel—this is—"

"Don't stop," she says, but there's amusement in her voice. "You can form complete sentences later."

I let out a shaky laugh. "Sorry, I just—"

"Rhett." Her hands frame my face. "Less talking. More moving."

"Bossy," I manage, but I push deeper, both of us gasping at the sensation.

"Breathe," she whispers when I go completely still, buried to the hilt.

"Right. Breathing. That's a thing people do." I realize I've been holding my breath and let it out in a rush.

She laughs, and the sound vibrates around me in a way that makes me see stars. "You're ridiculous."

"I'm overwhelmed," I correct. "There's a difference."

Focus, Caldwell. Don't pass out on your first time.

Inch by inch, I sink into her until I'm fully seated. We both go very still, adjusting to the sensation. She feels perfect around me—like her body was made for mine.

"How does it feel?" she asks softly.

"Incredible," I manage. "Better than I ever imagined."

"Harder," she breathes, wrapping her legs around my waist.

I increase my pace, driven by the way she responds to me. The bed creaks under our movement, and the sound mingles with our breathless gasps.

"You feel so good," I groan against her neck. "So tight. So perfect."

"Yes," she pants, her nails digging into my shoulders. "Just like that. Don't stop."

I shift my angle slightly, and when I hit that spot inside her, she cries out. Her pussy clenches around my cock, and I know I won't last much longer.

"Oh gods, Rhett," she gasps.

"Come for me," I murmur, reaching between us to find her clit. "Let me feel you come on my cock."

The combination of my words and my cock hitting that perfect spot inside her sends her over the edge. She comes with my name on her lips, her back arching, her pussy squeezing me so tight pushes me past the point of no return. I bury myself deep and come hard, her name torn from my throat as everything in me pours into her.

After, when we're both still catching our breath, I stay buried inside her, not ready to break the connection. The Ether has settled around us like a cocoon, silver and peaceful.

"That was—" I start, then stop, because there aren't words.

"Perfect," she finishes softly, tracing patterns on my chest.

I press my forehead to hers. "I never wanted anyone else. Only you."

We're both still breathing hard and wrapped around each other, as she traces patterns on my chest with gentle fingers.

"I'm still angry," she says quietly.

"I know."

"And I'm still figuring out how to trust you again."

"I know."

She presses a kiss to my collarbone. "But this—us—this is right. Even with everything else."

I tighten my arms around her, press my face into her hair. "Yeah. It is."

It's not forgiveness. It's not a promise that everything is fixed.

But I'll do anything to make sure I never lose her again.

Chapter 36
BREE

I wait until his breathing evens out, until I'm sure he's really asleep.

Rhett lies sprawled across my bed like he belongs there, one arm still curved around the space where I was lying. His face is relaxed in sleep, younger somehow, all the careful control he usually wears stripped away. The Ether has settled around him like a blanket, silver and peaceful.

Beautiful. He's so beautiful it makes my chest ache.

But I need space to think. To process what just happened between us, what it means, what I'm supposed to do with the tangle of emotions knotted up inside me.

I slip from the bed as quietly as I can, gathering my clothes from where they were scattered across the floor. The memory of how they got there—his hands shaking as he undressed me, mine fumbling with his belt—sends heat crawling up my throat. His warmth still clings to my skin, smoke and soap tangled in the sheets.

I leave it behind anyway.

I was waiting. For you. Always for you.

I dress in the bathroom, not trusting myself to be quiet if I do it in the bedroom. When I come out, he hasn't moved. Still sleeping, still beautiful, still making my heart do complicated things I don't want to think about.

I slip out the door and close it softly behind me.

The sanctuary is quiet in that deep way that only comes in the hours before dawn. My bare feet are silent on the cool stone as I make my way through the corridors, following a path I've walked so many times now it's become automatic. Past the kitchen, through the main hall, toward the entrance.

I need to see it again. The chamber. I need to understand what's waiting for me without everyone else's fear and protection clouding my judgment.

The heavy doors open silent at my touch. The sanctuary answers me without asking—the night air cool and honest against my skin.

I step outside and stop.

Mairen is sitting on the stone steps, wrapped in a soft shawl, like she's been waiting for me.

"Going to see her, then?" she says gently, not seeming surprised to see me.

I don't ask how she knows. Mairen was in the kitchen when Stellan and Thane told us about the Ashen Oath. She heard everything.

"I need to understand," I say simply.

She nods, not trying to stop me or call for the others. "Of course you do."

I should go. The chamber is calling to me, that pull I've been feeling since we left growing stronger in the quiet hours before dawn. But something about the way she's sitting there, patient and waiting, makes me settle beside her on the steps.

"You know about it," I say. It's not a question.

"Some." Her fingers adjust her shawl, and there's something in her expression—memory, maybe. "My grandmother used to tell stories. Old ones, passed down through our family line."

"About the Oath?"

"About the last one in our family who tried it." Mairen's voice is soft, thoughtful. "This was generations ago, mind you. Before the Council, before things were as structured as they are now."

I wait, sensing there's more.

"He was young," she continues. "Powerful. Full of certainty about what he wanted." Her smile is sad but not bitter. "Sound familiar?"

"What happened to him?"

"He chose fusion. Complete merging with his reflection." Mairen looks out at the garden, her eyes distant. "The power was extraordinary for a time—he could reshape reality with a thought. But power like that devours, and it didn't stop with him."

My chest tightens. "What do you mean?"

"He took everything. From everyone around him. It hollowed him out until nothing remained but hunger." Her voice carries more sadness than fear. "In the end, there wasn't anything left of the boy who walked into that chamber. Just the need for more."

The words settle between us, heavy but not threatening. Like she's giving me information, not trying to scare me away from my choice.

"Is that what you think will happen to me?" I ask quietly.

"Oh, dear." Mairen turns to look at me, her dark eyes kind but serious. "You're not him."

"How do you know?"

"Because you're here, asking questions instead of charging ahead. Because you care about the people who love you enough to worry about hurting them." She reaches over and takes my hand, her fingers warm and steady. "Because you're not doing this for power."

"Then why am I doing it?"

"Only you can answer that." Her smile is understanding. "But I suspect it's because you know you have to. Not because someone's forcing you, but because it's who you are."

I think about the chamber waiting for me, about Riley's face in the mirrors, about the choice that's been building since the moment I first touched the crown.

Mairen's gaze drifts across the small homes I built with Ether, families asleep inside—Feeders who found sanctuary here after centuries of injustice. Her voice softens. "And for them. To give them a fighting chance."

The weight of that responsibility settles on my shoulders, heavier than the choice itself. All these people who look to me, who believe I can somehow make things better. Maybe I can. Maybe that's what the Oath is really about.

"The guys will be furious that I went alone."

"Probably." Mairen's smile turns slightly mischievous. "But they'll understand eventually. Some things have to be faced alone first, before they can be shared."

She stands, brushing off her shawl. "My grandmother had one more thing to say about that story."

"What?"

"The boy who was consumed—he went in believing he knew exactly what he wanted. But he never asked her what she wanted." Mairen's eyes meet mine. "Maybe that was the real mistake."

The words hit something deep in my chest, a truth I hadn't considered. The mist around my feet stirs, responding to the shift in my understanding.

Riley is not a thing to be taken. She is someone to be asked.

"Don't make yourself smaller for anyone," Mairen says, echoing her earlier advice. "But don't forget that power shared is often stronger than power hoarded."

I stand, feeling steadier than I have in days but also more uncertain. "Thank you."

"No need for thanks. Just remember—whatever you choose in that chamber, make sure it's truly your choice. Not what others want from you, not what you think you should want. Yours."

I nod, then turn toward the path that leads away from the sanctuary. Away from Rhett sleeping in my bed, away from the others who would try to protect me from this.

Toward the chamber. Toward Riley. And whatever I'm meant to become.

"Bree," Mairen calls softly.

I turn back.

"Trust yourself. You're stronger and wiser than you know."

The words wrap around me like a blessing as I walk into the pre-dawn darkness, following the pull I can't ignore any longer.

The chamber has been waiting. So have I.

A cold breeze stirs the air around me, carrying something that feels like whispered promises. For just a moment, I swear I hear a voice—low, intimate, familiar.

"Trust yourself, Little Queen. Take what's yours."

Ethos's voice sends a shiver through me. But now, it feels like permission.

Like someone finally understands what I deserve.

Chapter 37
BREE

My heartbeat echoes in the silence, too loud as I stare at my reflection in the ornate mirror.

The frame is tarnished silver that flows in twisted curves and spirals, rising to sharp points like horns. It's almost identical to the hand mirror I found in the Sanctuary garden—the one that showed me eyes glowing red, then black as endless night. This one is larger, more elaborate, but unmistakably from the same source. The metal should be dirty after ages in this ancient chamber, but it's pristine, like someone just polished it moments ago.

In the glass, I see myself clearly. Dark hair tangled from earlier with Rhett, green eyes wide with fear and determination. Gray's oversized hoodie I threw on hangs loose on my frame, and there are shadows under my eyes from too little sleep and too much worry.

I look small. Ordinary. Nothing like someone who should be standing in this chamber trying to make the world different.

For just a moment, my reflection freezes. Not me—I'm still breathing, still shifting my weight from foot to foot. But the girl in the mirror goes completely still, like someone hit pause on just her.

And then she blinks.

I didn't.

Riley.

She looks like me, but different. Same dark hair, same green eyes, but she's wearing a crown—thin silver that catches the light. She stands up straighter than I ever do, like she's never wondered if she belongs somewhere.

But her hands are shaking.

She puts her hand against the glass from her side. Her mouth moves, but I can't hear anything.

"What do you want, Riley?"

The words just come out. I need to know.

"To be joined. To be whole, finally." Her voice sounds desperate, even though she's trying to hide it. Like she's been waiting forever for someone to ask.

I can see it now—she looks as lonely as I feel. She doesn't want power.

She just doesn't want to be alone anymore.

"She's right, Little Queen."

The voice slides into my head, cold and too close. Ethos. I can almost feel him behind me.

"Take her. Take everything. That's what power is."

Something dark threads through the mist around my feet, and for a second, I want to. The way Riley sounds matches exactly what he's whispering. It would be so easy to just reach out and—

No.

I look at Riley again, really look. Past the crown, past how perfect she seems. She's just a girl who doesn't know how to put herself back together.

Just like me.

I press my hand against the mirror. "No. I won't consume you. I won't make you disappear just so I can feel better."

Relief washes over her face, and suddenly she looks more like me than she ever has. Not some perfect version. Just Bree.

"Then we stay separate," she says quietly. "But together."

I nod.

We both put our hands flat against the glass. When I speak, she speaks with me:

"I swear to choose, and be chosen. To remain two, and yet one. To protect, and not consume."

The Ether explodes.

Light bursts everywhere—from the mirror, from the walls, probably from me. It's so bright I have to close my eyes. Every mirror in the chamber starts making this sound, like singing but deeper.

Then Ethos screams.

It's not just noise. It tears through everything, through my head, like something breaking apart. The mirrors shake, and it feels like glass is shattering inside my skull.

"NO!"

The word rips through me, followed by this horrible sound of pure rage. I hold on, keeping my hand pressed against the glass next to Riley's. She's actually smiling now—small but real.

The scream stops.

Everything goes quiet.

And in that silence, I know the choice was mine.

It always was.

THANK YOU

To my readers: You are the light that guides this story through its darkest moments. Thank you for following Bree deeper into the mirrors, for holding space for her struggles with power and identity, and for trusting me with your hearts as everything gets more complicated. Your messages about how these characters have become real to you, how their bonds give you hope for your own relationships—that's the magic that keeps me writing through the hardest scenes.

Thank you for staying with Bree as she learns that healing isn't linear, that sometimes you have to break before you can rebuild, and that the people who truly love you will wait while you figure out who you're becoming.

Thank you for loving Thane even when he makes terrible choices, for believing in bonds that transcend understanding, and for recognizing that sometimes the greatest act of love is stepping back when someone needs space to grow.

To anyone who has ever questioned their own reflection: Bree's journey through the mirrors is for you. You are not defined by your worst moments or your deepest fears. The parts of yourself you're afraid to face don't make you unworthy—they make you human.

To everyone who knows that sometimes love means making impossible choices: This one's for you.

To anyone learning that power without wisdom is dangerous, but wisdom without courage is useless: Bree sees you.

Here's to facing the hard truths, choosing authenticity over perfection, and discovering that sometimes the most powerful magic is learning to love all the pieces of yourself—even the broken ones.

Sneak Peek: Veil of Echoes

RHETT

Heat jolts awake under my skin before my brain catches up.

I open my eyes to see the sanctuary's runes falter—warmth ripped from the walls like someone snuffed out an ancient candle. My fire magic surges in response, wild and restless, and I'm fully awake in seconds.

The bed beside me is empty.

The sheets are cooling too fast, warmth being pulled from them by something unseen. No lingering scent on the pillow, no trace of how she'd curled against me after we'd finally collapsed into sleep, exhausted from everything that happened with the Oath.

She was here. She was definitely here when I fell asleep.

Now there's nothing.

I sit up, heart hammering. "Bree?"

My voice echoes strangely in her circular bedroom, like the space is bigger than it should be. The horned mirror she found weeks ago sits untouched on her dresser, only reflecting my panic. The reading nook where Theo usually plants himself is empty.

Even the air feels wrong—too still, too quiet.

"Bree!" I call louder, already throwing myself out of bed.

Nothing.

I grab jeans from the floor, pulling them on as I stride toward the door. The sanctuary's wrongness crawls up my spine like a warning. My hands are already warm, fire magic responding to my panic.

The common area is empty when I burst through her door. All the connecting bedroom doors are closed, the silence too thick.

"Bree!" The shout tears out before I can think.

I tear through their rooms—Wes tangled in sheets, jolting awake; Jace cursing as he rolls upright from sleeping upside down; Theo blinking groggily in his doorway; Gray standing next to his bed like he never even tried to sleep. Not one of them with Bree.

"What's happening?" Wes asks, voice rough.

"Bree's missing," Theo says, and something in his tone makes everyone pause.

"Missing how?" Jace demands.

"I don't know!" I'm pacing now, heat radiating from my skin. "She was there when I fell asleep, and now she's just—gone. No note, no trace, nothing."

"The sanctuary," Wes says suddenly. "It doesn't feel right."

He feels it too. The warm pulse of protection that's become as familiar as breathing is flickering like a dying flame.

We spread out through the common area, but before any of us can suggest where to search, voices drift from the main hallway. Low, urgent conversation.

I storm toward the sound, the others following behind me.

Thane and Stellan stand near the large windows overlooking the grounds, both fully dressed despite the early hour. They're talking in the kind of hushed tones that mean trouble, heads bent close together.

They look up when we appear—a pack of half-dressed, panicked men led by me in nothing but jeans and barely contained fire.

"She's not fucking here!" I announce before either of them can speak.

Thane goes completely still. "What do you mean she's not here?"

"I mean she's gone! Vanished! I've checked every room—"

"Where could she have gone?" Gray asks quietly.

"The chamber," Stellan breathes, cutting me off.

Something that feels a lot like dread creeps up my spine.

"No," Jace says immediately, taking a step back. "She wouldn't. Not alone. Not without—"

"She would," Thane says grimly. "If she thought it was her choice to make."

Stellan is already moving toward the corridor that leads deeper into the sanctuary. "She shouldn't do it alone. If she's taking the Oath, we have to stop her."

We follow him toward the back door that leads out to the garden—the path that winds deeper into the sanctuary grounds, toward the chamber. We move like a pack of wolves chasing the scent of our missing heart. Behind me, Theo's breathing changes like he's trying to force a vision. Wes's footsteps falter once, his hunger clearly gnawing at him. Jace's knives appear in his hands without him seeming to think about it. Gray and Thane walk behind us, watching for threats just in case.

The journey to the Chamber seems longer than it was yesterday, the shadows deeper. Almost like the Sanctuary grounds are trying to prevent us from getting there.

When we finally reach the chamber entrance, the door stands open.

Silver light spills out from within, brighter than it's ever been. But there's something else threading through it now—something darker that makes my fire magic recoil.

"Bree," I whisper.

We descend the stairs in single file, and I can feel the exact moment each of them sees her.

She stands before the largest mirror in the center ring, one hand pressed flat against the glass. Light radiates from the point of contact. Silver shot through with black, like ink bleeding through water. The kind we've become accustomed to since Bree's visit to the Void.

As we watch her Ether swirls around her feet, and it becomes completely inverted—black mist threaded with silver. It moves differently too, more controlled, more purposeful.

I pull my focus away from the unsettling Ether and focus on Bree. She looks different. She still looks like the Bree I know, but there's something about the way she holds herself. Straighter. More certain. Like someone who's never doubted her place in the world.

"Bree," I call out, but she doesn't turn.

Her reflection in the mirror flinches at something unseen just for a moment, but when I blink, it's gone.

Stellan makes a sound behind me—low, sharp, like recognition he doesn't want to name.

"What?" I demand, but he's already moving down the remaining stairs.

"Bree," Thane calls, his voice carrying command I've never heard before. "Step away from the mirror. Now."

That gets her attention. She turns, and when her eyes meet mine, something in my chest feels uneasy.

They're still green, still beautiful, but they hold confidence I've never seen before, never thought I'd see on Bree.

"You came," she says, and her voice sounds pleased rather than defensive. "Good. You should see this."

"See what?" Gray asks quietly. He's appeared beside me without my noticing, fully dressed and alert.

She turns back to the mirror, pressing both hands against the glass now. The light flares brighter, and her reflection moves completely out of sync with her actual movements.

"The completion," she says simply. "The choice I was always meant to make."

Flames dance under my skin, wild and restless. She stands in front of the mirror like she's finally found calm, and it terrifies me.

The black Ether around her feet pulses once, like a heartbeat, and every instinct I have screams that something isn't right.

The woman touching the mirror might look like Bree, might sound like Bree.

But she's not afraid.

And Bree is always afraid, just a little. It's part of who she is—the careful way she moves through the world, the defensive curl to her shoulders, the way she checks over her shoulder for threats that might be following.

This woman has none of that.

This woman looks like she's never been broken at all.

"Bree," I say carefully, "what happened to you?"

She glances back at me, and for just a moment, something vulnerable flickers in her expression. Like she's afraid I won't like what I see.

But then it's gone, replaced by that unfamiliar certainty.

"I became who I was always meant to be," she says.

The mirror pulses with dark light, and I realize with growing horror that we might be too late to stop whatever's happening.

But looking at her now—confident, transformed, finally unafraid—I can't tell if we've lost her to something terrible, or if she's right and she's finally found who she was always meant to be.

Continue Bree's journey in *Veil of Echoes.*

About the Author

Zora Stone writes romantasy with teeth: fierce heroines, protective men who'd burn the world for them, and enough emotional wreckage to keep things interesting. When she's not plotting betrayals or steamy chaos, she's drinking iced coffee, dodging laundry, or daydreaming about enchanted forests.

You can find her online at:

Website: ZoraStone.com

TikTok | Instagram: @ZoraStoneAuthor

And on Amazon and Goodreads.

Want behind-the-scenes chaos and sneak peeks? ZoraStone.com/Influencers

ALSO BY ZORA STONE

The Ether Chronicles

Crown of the Mist
Into the Ether
Ashen Oath
Veil of Echoes
Shattering the Void
To the Final End

Arcanum Academy

Shadows of Change
Shadows Rising
Shadows Found
Shadows Revealed